Princess
From
Another
Planet

PRiNCeSS
FROM
ANOtHER
PLaNet

Mindy Schanback

SCHOLASTIC INC.

New York Toronto London Auckland Sydney
Mexico City New Delhi Hong Kong Buenos Aires

FOR MY HUSBAND,
JEFFREY SCHANBACK,
MY ONE TRUE PRINCE.

ISBN 0-439-88958-8

12 11 10 9 8 7 6 5 4 3 2   6 7 8 9 10 11/0

Printed in the U.S.A.   40

First Scholastic printing, October 2006

PRiNCESS
FROM
ANOtHER
PLaNet

CHAPTER 1

My mother believes that she's the queen of Pan-nadeau. Pannadeau isn't a country. It's a planet. On the other side of the Milky Way galaxy.

When I was a little kid I believed everything my mother told me. I'd even tell people that I was a princess from another planet. But now I keep that information to myself. And, I'll share a hard-won popularity tip for you: It's a rare kid who wants to make friends with extraterrestrial royalty.

In fairy tales on planet Earth, princesses live in beautiful castles, have plenty of servants, and more outfits than Barbie. Sure, they get captured by fire-breathing dragons from time to time. And sometimes their fathers want them to marry an icky prince. Still, it's a pretty nice life.

On Pannadeau they must have a different set of fairy tales entirely. Because I live in a trailer, wear my cousin's hand-me-downs, and work in my father's so-called antique store.

My dad's shop is located in Beachswept, a picturesque town that was settled more than three hundred and fifty years ago. In those days the town made its money from the whaling industry. People used whale oil lamps, lit spermaceti candles (made from the head of the sperm whale, if you can imagine anything so disgusting), wore whalebone corsets, and, in their spare time, carved decorative designs called scrimshaw in whale teeth. Eventually, the entire community died of boredom.

Only kidding. What actually happened was worse. These products became so popular that the fishermen killed almost all the whales. This created a big economic problem for the citizens of Beachswept. And, the whales weren't too happy about it either.

Man and whale settled into a long, deep depression. Then several hundred years later Route 407 was built. Overnight, travel time from the city to Beachswept went from almost eight hours to under four, and our little community became a summertime hot spot.

Things also picked up for the whales. A ban on whaling caused their population to increase and today BlueGreen Tours, owned and operated by our very own Captain Bob—you've probably heard his radio commercials—makes a small fortune taking people to see them.

So, that's the scoop on my town. My personal story begins sometime in early June. School was over for the day and I was working in my father's shop. Business, which didn't start humming until summer vacation began, was dead as a whale, as we say here in Beachswept. Still, a girl's got to try.

I was busy attempting to sell our lone customer, a white-haired lady, an ancient brass trumpet. She was looking to buy it as a present for her newborn grandniece. Frankly, I can't imagine why anyone would want to buy an old horn for a new baby, but that wasn't my problem. My problem was to make the sale before the lady died of old age, which, from the way things looked, could happen at any second.

The customer, who was having a wonderful time shopping, wanted to stay in the store forever. I, on the other hand, had homework. Which is not to say that I planned on letting her leave without making a purchase. Unlike my mother, who was preoccupied with other things, I had a living to make.

"I don't know," the white-haired lady said in a soft, quivery voice. She fingered her necklace, a silver chain with a pendant that looked like it might have once been a large pearl hat pin.

"It's one of the finest pieces in the store," I said, running my hand along the trumpet's slightly dented bell. Unfortunately, that was the truth. Our antique store is called What's in Grandma's Garage? And, if you go by the stuff we sell, the answer is a lot of junk.

"Hmm," the old lady said, lifting it up to examine it more closely. She adjusted her rhinestone-studded, blue-framed glasses. "It's a little bent."

"Gives it character," I said in my most winning voice. "Only twenty dollars and it has such beautiful lines."

The front bell tinkled as my dad pulled open the screen door. It squeaked like crazy. "Gotta oil that door," he muttered. He said that about twenty-seven times a day.

Struggling with an oversized box, he staggered over to the counter and rested it on the edge. "Whew," he said.

"Big box," the old lady said. She looked curiously at my father. "Are you the proprietor?"

"Joseph Wright at your service," my dad said, wiping his rather dirty palm on his pants before reaching out to shake.

She took his hand in both of hers and squeezed it. "It's just wonderful to meet you," she said, smiling up at him.

"Er, thank you. Nice to meet you, too," my father said.

"I was just showing this lady our fabulous antique trumpet," I said, trying to keep the sale on track.

"You have a lovely daughter," the lady said, smiling at my father. "She reminds me so much of a girl I once knew. Also very special."

"She's a winner all right," Dad said.

"What's inside?" the woman asked, pointing to the carton.

"Lawn trolls," Dad said. Carefully, he lifted one out to show her.

"I love lawn trolls," the lady practically squealed. "I wonder . . ."

If I had to spend an hour looking at lawn trolls I would go insane. "Babies don't like lawn trolls," I said authoritatively.

The old lady pressed her lips together. "I hadn't heard that."

"My guess is that not too many people have," Dad said dryly.

I turned my attention back to the customer. "Your grandniece is going to love this horn," I said. "Why, when I was an infant I played all day long with a horn just like this one."

"Did you?" she said, beaming at me.

"And now I'm first horn at West Beach High School."

"First horn? My, my, my." She looked down at the trumpet again and her glasses fell off. She began feeling around the counter.

I handed them back to her and continued to improvise. "Soloist in Mozart's Eleventh. Concertina for Horn in F Major." I raised my hands in front of my lips and pretended to be playing the horn. "Dum de dum. Dum de dum."

"Sounds like 'Three Blind Mice,'" my father said, hoisting up the box and lugging it down the shop's narrow central corridor and through the moth-eaten old blanket that separated the retail area from the back.

Whoops. "It does, doesn't it? Our music teacher says that lots of modern songs are based on classical compositions." Our music teacher did say that, making it about the first true thing I had said in the last half hour.

"Well, well, well." The old lady held out a twenty-dollar bill. "I think I'll take it."

"It's thirty," I said, glancing back to make sure my dad was out of earshot.

"Sorry. I thought you said twenty." A smile played around the corners of the old lady's mouth while she rooted around in her ancient cloth hand-bag, finally pulling out a crumpled ten-dollar bill.

"Thank you," I said, wondering if I could have gotten away with saying forty. Since the horn was for a baby girl, I wrapped it in pale pink tissue paper, then tied a bright scarlet ribbon around the middle.

"It looks very festive," she said, taking the parcel. "Think they'll guess what it is?"

"Not in a million years." I had a sudden image of the new mother opening her baby gifts. Booties, a bib, tiny dresses, and, oh yes, an enormous old dented trumpet. "They will be surprised and amazed."

"And delighted, I hope."

"I hope so, too," I said sincerely, though I wouldn't count on it.

The old lady placed the package on the counter, then reached out and grabbed my hands. She pulled me forward and stared into my eyes. "It was a great pleasure to make your acquaintance, Gracie Wright," she said, bowing slightly. Then she took the package and practically ran out of the store.

"Hey, how do you know my name?" I called after her, but she didn't answer.

Dad shambled out of the back room. "So, daughter, I have a question. Since when do you play the trumpet? Oh, pardon me, first trumpet, if there is such a thing?"

I walked over to the cash register and punched it open. Inside was a small pile of bills. A very small pile. "I guess I just developed a fondness for food and shelter."

Dad reached out and gave me a squeeze. "You know, you worry too much for a fourteen-year-old."

I squeezed him back. "You know, you don't worry enough for a fifty-eight-year-old."

"I worry. But not that we won't have enough to eat or a place to live. I worry that my daughter won't grow up honest. I want you to be like, you know, whatshisname?" He paused for a second. "Abraham Lincoln." The last couple of nights he had been reading a book titled *Honest Abe* to my little brother.

"Does that mean I have to wear one of those stovepipe hats? 'Cause, you know, the other kids are going to laugh at me."

"You know what I mean."

I looked down at my clothing, hand-me-downs from my cousin Wren, and thought about the tiny room in our little trailer I shared with my younger brother. Then I thought about the riding lessons I wanted so badly.

"You don't have to worry about money. We'll always get by," Dad said.

"I don't want to just get . . ." I looked at my father and my voice trailed off. He was wearing a ripped T-shirt and faded, paint-stained pants. He hadn't shaved in a couple of days, his workroom was a mess, and he was a terrible businessman. Still, he sat up all night assembling the bicycle I got for Christmas, played endless games of checkers with my little brother, and made the almost eight-hour round-trip drive into the city just to get Mom some of the special beads she wanted.

"What?" he said, giving me an off-center grin.

I gave him a quick hug. "Nothing. Everything's fine, Dad. Really." To change the subject I asked him if he'd begun work on Ms. Fermone's dresser yet.

Dad ran another business in the back, repairing old furniture. He wasn't a particularly skilled craftsman, and he was so forgetful that he almost never finished a project on time. Still, he was cheap, so he had a steady group of customers who didn't seem to mind if their desk handles were slightly off center or the shade of varnish on their table didn't exactly match the one on their chairs.

"You promised to scrape and refinish it by Friday," I reminded him.

"I've got a few dressers in the back. Tell me which one belongs to Ms. Fermone again."

"I didn't see the dresser because you picked it up while I was at school. But I remember her, because she was the lady who admired your biceps."

Dad blushed. "I remember now."

"I bet."

"Hey, I can't help that she liked me. Anyway, you know I'm committed to your mother."

"She's the one who ought to be committed," I mumbled.

All the friendliness went out of Dad's tone. "What's that?" he said coldly.

I knew better than to repeat that remark. "Nothing," I said, dropping my eyes.

I love my mother. I really do. But it's not easy being the daughter of a woman who thinks she's an alien queen. Especially since she got it into her head that the Maluxziads are coming. Coming to attack.

CHApTER 2

By the time we closed up the store, I managed to sell a silver-plated saltshaker, a Fourth of July serving dish, and a box of old medicine bottles made out of colored glass. In between customers I rearranged some shelves and wrote out a schedule of what my father needed to repair by when. So that he wouldn't lose it, I used almost half a box of pushpins to tack it onto the corkboard behind his workbench.

After that, I did my math homework and wrote a poem for language arts. My teacher had instructed us to come up with a short verse about an exciting event. I wrote about alien warriors conquering Earth:

Oh. No.

Last breath. Death.

Silence.

I read it to my dad, who agreed that it was short.

At six o'clock I locked up the store, then waited while Dad pulled our ancient truck around. We rattled down Main Street, made a left at the movie theater, and crossed over Pond Swamp Road into the fancy section of town.

I flipped on the radio. "The two teens killed in a robbery gone wrong had their brains stolen from the county morgue this morning. Police are investigating a connection between them and Bubba and Elroy, a pair of goats found dead on Greenlong Estates yesterday. Like the teens, the goats' brains had been surgically removed and taken away."

"*Gross,*" I said.

Dad shifted in his seat. "Ow!" he howled.

"What?"

Dad put his hand into his pocket and pulled out the list I had written earlier. It still had about ten pushpins in it.

"See these pushpins," I said in an exasperated voice.

"I don't need to see them," Dad said. "I've got one stuck in my thigh."

"I put them in so that the list would stay on the corkboard at the store," I said slowly. "That way you'd know what piece of furniture was due when."

"I think I have some varnish and finishing nails at home, and I wanted to have the list so that I could remember what I needed to bring back."

It sounded convincing. But I knew from experience that Dad would either lose the list, forget the stuff he wanted to bring to the store, or come up with some ingenious but impracticable home project that involved pushpins.

I sighed. Sometimes I didn't even know why I tried.

The truck bumped onto Great Barrier Road, a street lined with oaks so ancient they practically had age spots. We turned through a pair of heavy iron gates marked Baldwin. A gigantic brick mansion set on a perfectly trimmed green lawn loomed ahead of us. About a hundred yards down, the driveway split. We took the right-hand fork. Almost immediately it turned into a rutted dirt trail that led back to the edge of the property. There, in a little clearing, stood our home, a dilapidated trailer.

Dad pulled in behind the trailer, next to a rough wooden picnic table covered with gardening supplies and vegetable seedlings, two nonworking televisions, and a bucket filled with corroded bolts, screws, and nails that he had been promising to sort for the last ten years. Also littering the area were several stacks of lumber, a barbecue grill with one wheel missing, a pile of assorted ceramic tiles, a small heap of rusty doorknobs, an abandoned baby stroller, a bicycle with no handlebars, an avocado-colored sink, a broken lawnmower, an ancient fishing reel, and a speckled marble countertop that didn't fit anything.

"Okay, Princess," Dad said as the truck engine gave its final cough and shudder, "we're home."

"I'm not a princess," I said, opening the door.

Before I could get out of the truck, my five-year-old brother, Chuck, shot out of the trailer door and ran over to me. Wearing nothing but a terry cloth robe and flip-flops, he jumped up holding his arms in the air like a karate master.

"Ah, wah!" Chuck yelled. He ran through some moves, whipping his arms around and kicking the air. It didn't look exactly like he was performing a martial art. More like he was having a spasm.

"Wo, wo, wo!" he screamed, crouching down low with his arms raised. He looked so ready for action that it was all I could do not to laugh.

I held my arms up and brought my foot around, gently tapping his rear end. "Ah, rah," I said back.

Chuck brought his head down and charged, butting me in the belly. I grabbed him under his arms, spun him around, then lifted him up. He wrapped his legs around my middle and hugged me. "Who are you today?" I asked Chuck, squeezing him tightly.

"Karate Man, Prince of Punishment."

"He's very scary," I said.

"He won't hurt you if you give him a pretzel."

"Oh, really." I carried him into the trailer. "We're going to Cousin Wren's birthday dinner tonight, so only one. Okay?"

"Okay."

I gave him a pretzel stick.

16

Dad showed up behind us. "What about me?" he asked.

"We're going to Cousin Wren's birthday dinner tonight, so only one. Okay?"

"Do I look like I'm five?" Dad asked.

"Not too many gray five-year-olds," I said.

"Though mostly you're bald," Chuck added helpfully.

Dad took a handful of pretzel sticks, sticking one in his mouth and jamming the rest into his pocket.

"Only one," Chuck said.

"If I have to eat one of your aunt Leora's, what do you call 'em, gourmet dinners, I'd just as soon fill up on pretzel sticks. Remember what we had last time? Something sea-urchin-disgusting something."

"Roasted and shredded sea-urchin ragout."

"Right." He shuddered.

I handed Chuck another pretzel and took one for myself.

"Birthday cake," Chuck yelled.

"I'm sure they'll have that," I said, bending down to kiss his head, which smelled like shampoo and baby powder. Chuck looked just like Dad except for his coloring, which was Mom's all over. He was stocky and had a round, chubby face with high color, a light sprinkling of freckles, large wide-spaced eyes, and thick tawny hair.

I was just the opposite, petite and slender with delicate features like my mom, except that I had my father's darker coloring and curly black hair.

I heard the hair dryer switch off in my parents' bedroom. "Hey, Mom," I called out, knocking on the door.

"The Magnificent Presence permits you to enter."

I cracked open the door. My mother, Dorothea Quicksilver Wright, was looking into a chipped mirror while putting on earrings. She was wearing a calf-length flowered dress that highlighted her wide hazel eyes. Her long honey-colored hair was piled up on top of her head and her makeup was perfect.

I walked into the bedroom. "You look lovely, Mom," I said.

"Thank you, dear," she said in her musical voice. "Don't forget to curtsy."

Chuck came in behind me sucking on his pretzel. When he saw Mom, he took the pretzel out of his mouth and gave her a short, stiff bow.

I had given up curtsying to my mother years ago. When I was little I practiced until I had, in my mother's words, "the best curtsy this side of Polaris." To execute the perfect curtsy, you hold your arms gracefully in second position. Then you place your right toe behind your left heel, bending down your head, and do a deep knee bend with your left knee, using your right heel as a balance. Then you lift yourself up, holding your back straight and dropping your arms in a simple elegant line. Done correctly, it's as beautiful as a butterfly.

My mother lifted her chin and looked in the mirror. "Technically, this is the birthday of a relative, which is a state occasion requiring a crown."

I definitely didn't want my mother to wear that little circlet of rhinestones she called her crown to my cousin's birthday party. As it was, Aunt Leora thought my mother was nuts. "Informal is very chic, very now," I said firmly. I even hoped it was true.

"Those who show up at a state affair looking as if they belong at a ball game tend to strike out socially," Mom said. "But as Wren is only a Minor Miss perhaps it would be a tad ostentatious."

"Oh yes," I said, quickly seizing the opportunity, "more than a tad."

"A whole tadpole," Chuck said. He finished his pretzel stick. "I command another pretzel."

Dad walked into the bedroom and bowed almost imperceptibly to Mom. "Wow," he said, looking her over. "I can't believe I married someone so gorgeous."

And it was hard to believe. Mom was so beautiful and graceful and elegant, while Dad was, well, whatever the opposite of beautiful, graceful, and elegant was.

Mom smiled fondly at Dad. "You, Gallant Consort, are filthy."

Dad looked down and rubbed his three-day growth of stubble. "I'm Filthy Man," he sang in a deep voice.

"I'm Karate Man!" Chuck yelled.

Dad bounded up, landing on the balls of his feet with his arms in fighting stance. "Let us battle to the death," he said.

"Let us leave the room," I said to Mom.

"Charles is clean and I'd like him to stay that way," Mom said to Dad. "And you need a shave and a shower."

The males, now engaged in hitting and grunting, completely ignored her.

"Maybe we should just throw in a hunk of meat and go to the party without them," I suggested to Mom.

"I'm not going to visit Dad's sister without him. That woman is as mad as a hatter," Mom said indignantly. She turned her attention to me, clasping her elegant, long-fingered hands together across her chest. "And what about you? What are you wearing to tonight's soiree? Your yellow dress?"

"I don't want to wear anything that used to belong to Wren."

Wren was a few months younger than me, but several inches taller. That, plus the fact her mother buys her enough clothing to outfit a small nation, makes me one of the best-dressed girls at West Beach High School. Wren doesn't even go to West Beach High. Her parents send her to Whitmore Prep, a private academy.

"Don't forget that whatever you wear, you are Gracie Quicksilver Wright, Royal Miss of the Southern Seas and the Premier Princess of Pannadeau, while your cousin is only a Minor Miss without a drop of royal blood," Mother said.

"Then how come she gets to live in the castle?" I joked. Wren's house was about the size of the Taj Mahal.

"Living in a castle doesn't make you a princess any more than living in a burrow makes you a rabbit. Perhaps I should wear my crown."

"Can't argue with that logic." I stole a look at my watch and jogged out of Mom's room and into the room I share with Chuck. I threw on a pair of good-quality linen pants and an elegant silk-satin blouse with a rip at the bottom. The whole outfit cost only $3.75 because I bought it at a garage sale. If I ever get rich, I thought, buttoning up the blouse, everything I buy will be brand new.

Carefully, I tucked in the shirt so that the rip didn't show and secured it with a wide leather belt. I fluffed up my short dark hair, adjusted my rectangular tortoiseshell glasses, and was ready to rock.

When Dad and Chuck were dressed to Mom's satisfaction, we set out. We crossed the lawn and walked up the white stone path that led to the mansion. It was an enormous redbrick affair that had more than its share of turrets. My aunt had just finished another renovation, this time adding a pair of squat towers to each end of the house.

Mom shuddered. "Ugh. It gets more hideous every year."

"I like it," Dad said. "It says something."

"And what it says is, I have terrible taste," Mom replied, adjusting the rhinestone circlet that adorned her hair.

"A woman going to a casual family dinner with that thing on her head shouldn't talk about taste," I said.

"It's not a thing. It's the mark of royalty," Mom said.

I don't know what's gotten into Mom lately. She's always thought she was the queen of Pannadeau, but for years she barely mentioned it. The idea just sat there, not really accepted by Dad and myself, but not talked about either, like the broken door handle on the refrigerator. Then a couple of months ago she started getting bad vibes from outer space, and suddenly her royal status on the other side of the galaxy was a big topic of conversation.

"I am Pannadeau," Mom said in her most regal voice.

"I am Charles Thurston Quicksilver Wright," Chuck yelled.

"The Royal Master of the Northern Ports and the Premier Prince of Pannadeau," Mom added.

"Try to say something nice about the house," Dad said. "You know how insecure my sister is."

"That's true. She is without a doubt the most insincere person I ever met."

"Dotty," Dad said in a low voice. It was a clear warning.

"Don't worry about me. I'll be my usual gracious self," Mom said.

"It would go better if you'd consider being your unusual silent self," Dad said, softening his words with an affectionate pat and a smile.

Together we mounted the steps. "Let's all remember the concept of noblesse oblige," Mom said grandly.

I knew all about noblesse oblige, the obligation of royalty to be gracious to their social lessers. For a moment we stood at the door.

"It's showtime," I said.

"Okay," Dad said. "Please, for once, everyone, let's try to have a pleasant evening at my sister's."

CHAPTER 3

"You may ring the doorbell now, Charles," Mom said.

Chuck pushed the button and the doorbell played a tune. "Merrily, merrily, merrily, merrily, life is but a dream," he sang along.

Mom sighed. "They're such plebeians," she said.

I caught Chuck's questioning look. "It means common people," I whispered, just as Blanca, Aunt Leora and Uncle Thomas's housekeeper, opened the door.

"Hi, Blanca," Chuck said. "Are you a penguin, too?"

"I am Costa Rican," Blanca said.

"That's plebeian," I whispered to Chuck.

"I like penguins better," Chuck said.

"So do I," Mom said behind us.

Aunt Leora, Wren, and a girl about her age were gathered in the living room. My aunt rose when we came in. "I'm so happy you could come to celebrate this wonderful occasion," she said in a fake over-enthusiastic voice, "for there is nothing quite like family."

"There's nothing quite like malaria either," Mom said to me under her breath. She smiled at my aunt, and in a louder voice complimented her on her outfit before wishing Wren a happy birthday.

Dad went to give Aunt Leora a hug and kiss, but she moved away slightly and he ended up kissing the air.

No one would ever guess by watching them that my father raised Aunt Leora from the time she was three years old, after their parents died in a car accident. He acted like a father to Wren and her older brother, Pierce, too, as Uncle Thomas was almost always away on business.

Dad went over to Wren. "Happy birthday." He gave my cousin a hug and handed her a small brightly wrapped box.

"Thanks, Uncle Joe," Wren said, but before she could even give the box a shake, her mother grabbed it out of her hand.

"Presents will be opened after dinner with the cake," Aunt Leora said tartly, taking the packages Chuck and I were holding.

"She's cranky because she's a penguin, right?" Chuck asked Mom in a loud whisper.

"Have you met Ann Armstrong?" Aunt Leora asked me.

"I don't know," I said, smiling at the girl with the shiny brown hair and a nose that was definitely not made by God. "You look awfully familiar, though," I said, extending my hand.

Ann looked up but didn't reach out to shake.

After a second I dropped my hand to my side. "Did you go to Town Camp last summer?" I tried again.

"I wouldn't dream of going to a dreary place like Town Camp. My mother sent me to the Moshulu Sailing Institute in Maine."

"I can quite see why she wanted to get rid of you," I said.

"Ann and Wren are working on a school project together," Aunt Leora said, shooting me a venomous look.

"About the nature of protoplasm," Wren said. "It's real interesting because—"

"You know, you're wearing my sister's clothes," Ann said, cutting Wren off.

My stomach contracted as I remembered where I had seen Ann Armstrong before. It was at the garage sale where I bought this outfit. "Don't be ridiculous."

"I recognize that shirt. It has a little rip along the bottom seam. I know because I ripped it. Let me show you." Ann reached for the shirt and I stepped back.

"Gracie and I bought that shirt together at the Bayside Mall," Wren said. "I remember because I wanted one, too, but there weren't any in my size."

My cousin was a true pal.

"Look, Chuck," Wren said, trying to change the subject. "We got a new fish." She gestured to the huge fish tank that dominated the room. "See the white one with the gigantic eyes and red head. It's a red-capped, bubble-eyed gold."

Chuck, who loved Uncle Thomas's exotic gold-fish, trotted over to the tank followed by Mom, who was muttering, "Big eyes, red head," to herself. Mom gazed into the tank then let out a scream.

Everybody jumped. I ran over to the tank. Mom, who had a frozen expression on her face, was pointing at a two-inch-long fish with eyes that popped out from either side of its head like two oversized donuts. It was all white except for a bright red mark on the top of its head.

"Kill it immediately," Mom said.

"No," Chuck cried. "It's a nice fish."

"Kill it?" Aunt Leora yelled. "My husband paid a fortune for that fish."

Mom cupped her hands around her eyes and stared into the tank. "Oh," she said in a totally different tone. "My mistake. It can live."

"Excellent," Aunt Leora said in an acidic voice. "I'm delighted you have spared my fish."

"My fault entirely," Mom said graciously. "I didn't notice it lacked antennae."

"What lacks antennae?" Pierce, Wren's older

brother and the most popular boy at Whitmore Prep, asked, walking into the room. He was wearing mud-spattered sweatpants and had a lacrosse stick slung over his shoulder. Like my dad whom he resembled, Pierce was of below average height and stocky, with curly black hair and untroubled brown eyes. The atmosphere in the room immediately lightened.

"Long story," I said.

"Whoops," he said, looking around the room. "I see it's time for Wren's birthday dinner. I'll be back in a flash." Pierce turned and tore up the stairs, appearing a few minutes later in a collared sports shirt and chinos. Grinning from ear to ear, he greeted everyone warmly. Ann, who got all flustered when Pierce said hello to her, could barely get out a sentence.

Pierce handed his sister some crumpled brown paper with masking tape on it. "Happy birthday, sis," he said brightly.

"Thanks," Wren said, smiling. "I see you wrapped it yourself."

"It's not as easy as it looks," Pierce said cheerfully. "It's a video. *Famous Moments in Sports.* We'll watch it after dinner. Okay?"

"I love moments in sports, famous ones especially," Ann said, blushing furiously.

"Hey, great," Pierce said, smiling.

"Yeah," Ann said, dropping her pocketbook. "Wow."

Dinner was scallops poached in a balsamic vinegar sauce with pureed pears and almonds. Dad stuck his entire portion of scallops under one of the extra rolls he took from the bread basket.

All Aunt Leora could talk about was the camp she had just signed up Wren for this summer. She must have said it was very exclusive about a hundred times. That's a code word for expensive.

Camp Greenlong, part of a humongous estate, was owned by a Lady Gregson, the eldest daughter of a duke and a Swedish princess—and this was where my aunt started to drool—the cousin of Queen Mirabella. Apparently, everybody who was anybody wanted to make friends with Lady Gregson and be invited to the tea she had for the royal family every fall. But Lady Gregson, a passionate gardener and horsewoman, never joined committees or accepted invitations, choosing only to socialize with her royal relatives. Not that that kept the society ladies from Beachswept County from trying.

"Sounds like things worked out well for her," my mother commented, causing Aunt Leora to go on for another twenty minutes about Lady Gregson's social pedigree.

The conversation was so boring that I was about to fall into my pureed pears. Then Aunt Leora mentioned riding. Not only did Camp Greenlong have water skiing, sailing, and canoeing, but each kid was assigned a horse and got to ride every day.

Ann looked really interested but Wren, who was twirling her hair like she always did when she got nervous, put one hand around her neck, and stuck out her tongue like she was strangling herself.

Poor Wren. My cousin's idea of a good time was to curl up by herself with a good book. She wasn't wild about people, hated sports, and only liked animals if they were either far enough away to be sketched or small enough to be seen under a microscope.

I, on the other hand, loved horses and had been wanting to ride since I was little. Once I even got Dad to order a bunch of brochures from the local riding schools. But when I saw how expensive the lessons were, I pretended to lose interest.

Dad caught Wren making a face. "You don't want to go, Wren?" he asked gently.

"Of course she wants to go," Aunt Leora said. "She's looking forward to it."

"It sounds like a wonderful place," Ann said enthusiastically.

"As you know, I wanted to go to science camp," Wren said.

"And look at dreary test tubes all day," Aunt Leora said.

"Right now, I'm interested in wild bird migrations. Twice a year five billion birds take off and travel to another place."

"Sure wouldn't want to be under them," Pierce said.

Ann, who had been sneaking looks at Pierce throughout the meal, burst into peals of laughter. "You are so funny," she said, leaning forward and putting her elbow directly into her dinner plate.

I burst out laughing and she glared at me.

"So, Gracie," Pierce said, "what are you doing this summer?"

"I'm going to help out in the store and take care of Chuck."

"I want you to spend some time enjoying yourself, too," Dad said. "You do enough work."

"And you," Aunt Leora said, pointing her fork at Pierce, "don't do enough."

"What do you mean?" Pierce asked.

"I heard from your English teacher today, young man, and you never handed in your biography paper."

"Oh yeah," Pierce said unhappily.

"And your social studies teacher isn't too happy with you either. If you can't get your work done, you're going to have to go to summer school," Aunt Leora said.

"What about my sports camp?" Pierce yelped. Pierce, who was in constant danger of flunking out, was a terrific athlete.

"School comes first," Aunt Leora said.

Dad interrupted. "Maybe you and Pierce could speak to his teachers and find out exactly what he's missing. Then he can make it up over the summer."

"Maybe," Aunt Leora said, nodding.

Pierce mouthed the words *thank you* across the table to Dad.

Wren opened her presents as soon as the birthday cake was served. Aunt Leora bought her some beautiful clothes: buttery suede shorts, a red denim jacket, a couple of summer blouses, a pretty sundress, and a pair of wonderful leather riding boots. Wren smiled nicely and said thank you, but I knew she really wanted the new illustrated five-volume bird encyclopedia.

My parents gave her a silver filigree bracelet she'd admired at the store. I bought her a book about drawing from nature, and Chuck had made her a paper airplane that he decorated with stickers.

"I'll give you my present at your party," Ann said.

"The party I was invited to stay away from?" Pierce said, smiling.

"No, you can come," Ann said.

I went still. No one had invited me to Wren's party. I tried to catch my cousin's eye, but she didn't look up, not even when I kicked her under the table.

After dinner Pierce and Chuck went outside to

toss a baseball around—Pierce was the captain of the Whitmore baseball team—and Aunt Leora asked my dad to come look at some damaged tiles in one of the downstairs bathrooms. I started upstairs to Wren's room to retrieve a sweater. As I passed the hall to the bathroom I heard my father and aunt arguing. Instead of making a right turn up the stairs, I tiptoed down the hall to listen.

"Really, Joe," Aunt Leora was saying. "Anyone with eyes can see that the situation is deteriorating."

"Things seem about the same to me," Dad said. "And you have to admit that she was absolutely fine tonight."

"Except for wearing that circlet of rhinestones she calls her crown."

"It's a whatchamacallit." Dad said, "A fashion statement."

"Oh really, and I suppose her desire to kill my husband's prize goldfish was a subtle endorsement of the death penalty." Aunt Leora paused for a second. "Have you spoken to her old doctor at Barking Tree? Maybe she should go back for a little, uh, rest."

"She's fine, Leora."

"You're blind to this issue, and it's not good for you or your kids."

"All right. Enough." Dad popped out of the bathroom. "Kids," he yelled, not seeing that I was standing in the hall.

"Right here," I said. "Just getting my sweater from Wren's bedroom."

"Which is up the stairs in the opposite wing of the house," Dad said tartly.

"Well, it's a big place," I said senselessly. "So"—I grabbed Dad's arm—"were you and Aunt Leora talking about Mom?"

"I was talking to an adult about adult things. Go get your sweater and your brother. We have to go."

At least we had gotten through the evening without Mom saying anything too crazy. Everyone but Pierce was gathered at the door saying good-bye when Ann stopped my mother. "Excuse me, Mrs. Wright," Ann said, "but I was wondering if you could tell me how to identify aliens?"

"It's like anything else," Mom said. "Practice and experience."

"We've got to go," I said, quickly opening the door. "I have some homework to finish by bedtime. Come on, Mom."

Ann began making a weird hooting sound. "What about *oooooooo*?" she asked. "Is that an alien sound?"

My mother stared at Ann. "Could be," she said. "Why?"

"Just something I heard."

"Well, if you heard anything, it's your duty to tell the Magnificent Presence," my mother said.

"We have to go," I said firmly.

"How about *woo-woo-woo*?" Ann asked.

"Cut it out, Ann," Wren said.

Mom turned white. "Gracie, I told you I'd been getting bad vibrations lately."

"She's just making it up, Mom."

"No, really. I heard them," Ann said.

Suddenly noblesse oblige went out the window. "Shut up," I said to Ann. "Just shut up."

"Gracie Wright, apologize this instant," Aunt Leora said.

"Let *her* apologize," I said hotly.

Mom threw herself into Dad's arms. "Joseph,

they're here. They're here and they want the children." She pointed at Ann. "This girl heard them."

Eyes blazing, Dad took a step toward Ann.

"I was just kidding around," Ann said quickly. "I didn't mean to upset you, Mrs. Wright."

A horn sounded outside.

Mom held herself up straight. "We will pardon you this time."

"That's my mom. Tell Pierce I said good-bye," Ann said, moving swiftly toward the door.

"You can tell him yourself," Pierce said, walking back into the room. "Bye, Ann."

"Yeah," Ann said, walking squarely into the door. "Forgot to open it. Silly me. Bye, Pierce." She fled.

"This is exactly what I was talking about," Aunt Leora said to my father.

"Wren," Dad said. "You didn't know about this?"

"Of course not. You know I'd never do anything mean to Aunt Dotty. And Gracie is my best friend."

"How did Ann know about the aliens then?" Dad asked.

Wren went white and her eyes filled with tears. "Sorry, Aunt Dotty," she said. She turned on her heel and fled up the stairs.

Mom regained her composure. "Thank you for a lovely dinner," she said.

Dad lifted Chuck onto his shoulders and opened the door. Head held high, Mom swept grandly from the house. Her circlet of rhinestones sparkled under the outdoor lights.

"See you on Saturday, Gracie," Pierce said.

Aunt Leora cleared her throat and shook her head slightly at my cousin.

"Don't worry, Ma, I'm not going to contaminate your party," Pierce said with a grin.

"Me either," I said, walking out of the house.

Dad, with Chuck on his shoulders, took Mom's hand. I followed behind. We were each lost in our own thoughts as we crossed the lawn and headed back to our trailer.

CHAPTER 4

It wasn't until the next day that I had the idea. The wonderful, fabulous, incredible idea. I was snoozing in my favorite spot, a large, flat rock behind the azaleas. I was supposed to be studying my social studies text, but the day was warm and the book was dull. Unlike my cousin Wren, I find most books boring, which probably explains why school is not my best subject. I was awakened by the sound of Aunt Leora talking to Wren.

"Smaller bites, Wren, and pat your mouth with a napkin in between bites."

I sat up and peered out through the azaleas. Aunt Leora and Wren were sitting at a little table on the lawn set with cloth napkins and real silver. In the middle of the table sat a three-tiered silver plate loaded with tiny sandwiches, scones with butter and jelly, mini muffins, and little cakes.

"These petits fours are just glorious, aren't they?" Aunt Leora said.

I popped my head out of the bushes like a periscope. Aunt Leora had her back to me, but Wren gave me a little wave.

"Don't wave about. And take tiny sips. It's not ladylike to slurp," Aunt Leora said.

I made a face and scratched under my arms like a monkey. Wren smiled into her cup.

"Speak, Wren. Sometimes conversing with you is like talking to a wall."

"I'm reading a book about Madame Curie. She won the Nobel Prize twice," Wren said.

"That's interesting," Aunt Leora said in a bored voice. "Whom did you have lunch with at school today?"

Wren twirled her long white-blonde hair. "One for physics, that one was with her husband, Pierre, and a French physicist named Antoine Henri Becquerel. The other one was in 1911 for chemistry."

"You ate alone again, didn't you?" Leora sighed, shaking her head sorrowfully.

"Look. There's Gracie," Wren said to distract her.

Aunt Leora swiveled around. "Afternoon, Gracie," she called. "Why don't you come and join us for tea?"

"Love to," I said, walking over then leapfrogging into the empty chair between my cousin and aunt.

I reached out to grab one of the little iced cakes, but she blocked my wrist with a small perfectly manicured hand.

"Wait for silverware, Gracie. Good table manners are very important."

"Not starving to death is even more important," I said.

"Isn't this lovely? My two favorite girls to tea," Aunt Leora said. She patted her lips lightly with a napkin and rang the little silver bell that sat on the table. A minute later, Blanca, dressed in a white uniform with a black apron, came out. "Could you set a place for Gracie please. And bring some of the supermarket cookies, too."

Blanca nodded and returned a few minutes later with another cup and a plate with some wafers on it. She set it down in front of me.

"How come I can't have what you're having?" I asked my aunt.

"Direct questions like that are impolite. The proper response to refreshment of any kind is 'thank you.' But clearly I didn't expect your company, so I bought only a small amount."

I looked at the piles of pastries and little sandwiches stacked high on the three-tiered tray. "I see," I said.

"They're for Pierce and his Whitmore friends, too." Aunt Leora lifted her fork and stabbed a piece of golden crust from a lemon-cherry tart. "Mmm. The Asterium Dance Company is performing at the Bayside Arts Center tonight, Gracie. Is your mother taking you?"

When I left Mom, she was sitting on the floor of her closet with a flashlight, riffling through a box of crystals she called her amulets and muttering to herself. So, it seemed unlikely. "She hasn't mentioned it," I said diplomatically.

"They are doing a modern piece about life in

the computer age, set to electronic music. Anna-belle Whippenforth, she's in charge of the fund-raising committee at the center, saw it and said it was acute and original."

"Indeed," I said. "Indeed" was what my father always said when he didn't understand what the other person was talking about.

"Excuse me," Aunt Leora said, getting up. "I must go and supervise as Blanca lays the table for dinner."

"How do you supervise someone laying the table for dinner?" I asked as soon as my aunt was out of earshot.

"And today, Blanca," Wren said, imitating her mother perfectly, "I want you to lay the knives diagonally across the plate. That's the way Mrs. Rockefeller-Carnegie-Astor-Mellon-Forbes the Third, she's the head of the Objects for People Too Poor to Decorate Their Homes As Tastefully As Old Money Would Commission, is doing it this year."

"Stop," I said, giggling. I grabbed one of the petits fours and took a bite. "Yum. Delicious."

"I can't take it anymore," Wren said in her own voice. "I could deal with her being obsessed with making friends with the right people herself. But now she wants me to make friends with the right people, too."

"Of which I'm obviously not," I said coolly.

"Oh, Gracie," she said softly. "You know I wanted to invite you to my party. Mom didn't want me to because Susan Howe and Loretta Richmond were coming."

"And I'd, what? Not say the right thing? Dress improperly? Pick my nose? Pollute the air?"

Wren dropped her eyes. "I'm sorry."

"You should be."

"She just runs right over me."

"What's her problem, anyway? That we live in a trailer? That my mother isn't on the right committees?"

Wren hung her head, too embarrassed to say anything.

"And you shouldn't have said anything to Ann about my mother," I continued angrily.

"I know. It's just . . ." Wren paused, gathering her thoughts. "It's just that I don't have anything to say to those girls. And your mother and the aliens are so interesting. I never thought Ann would actually meet her. Or you." Her eyes misted over and her delicate pale skin turned blotchy. "I love your mother. I really do. And now she probably hates me."

"No, she doesn't."

"Will you tell her I'm sorry?" She wiped her eyes with her hand.

I nodded. "I guess."

"Thanks." Wren sniffed. "Ever wonder if she's right?"

"I guarantee you that my mother didn't come to Earth through a wormhole, that she is not the queen of the planet Pannadeau even if there is a planet Pannadeau, which I sincerely doubt, and furthermore, there are no such things as Maluxziads and they are not, I repeat, are not out to get her!"

"Okay."

"Can we change the subject?" I asked.

"I wish I didn't have to go to that stupid camp," Wren burst out.

"Well, at least it's just in the morning." Aunt Leora had signed Wren up for the half-day program so that she could work on her piano in the afternoon.

"I know I'm going to hate it."

"I'd kill to go to a camp like that."

"It's funny, huh?" Wren said glumly. "You'd kill to go and I'd kill not to."

We looked at each for a minute. I nodded my head yes.

Wren shook her head no.

"Are you thinking what I'm thinking?" I asked excitedly.

"I'm definitely, positively not," Wren said, shaking her head so hard her long blonde hair whipped back and forth.

I bounced up and down with enthusiasm. "You are. You absolutely are."

"Anyway, there's no way we could get away with it."

I rested my chin on my hands. "Maybe, I could just come to the gates in the morning and get on the camp bus."

"Mom got a special deal on a limousine."

"Excellent," I squealed. "I love limousines."

"You've been in a limousine?"

I tossed my head. "Sure. What do you think, that I'm a lymphocyte?"

"You mean neophyte. A neophyte is a beginner and a lymphocyte is a blood cell."

"You better stay home and read some more," I said.

Wren glanced at her watch. "I've got to go and practice the piano." She pushed her chair away from the table. "It's a great fantasy, but we'd never get away with it. For one thing, my mother would probably notice that I was home."

"No, she wouldn't. We'd meet by the gates in the morning. I'd get into the limousine and you'd go to the tree house. While I was at Camp Greenlong riding the big, mean-tempered, scary horses who buck and kick and bite and smell bad, swimming in the deep, icy lake filled with icky fish and algae and dead sea horses—"

"Sea horses live in salt water."

"Dead other stuff, making conversation with girls just like Ann but even snootier and more disgusting, you'd be in the tree house all by yourself."

"Mmm." Just thinking about it made Wren smile.

I was making progress. "Writing notes for your bird journal, reading, sketching."

Wren sighed. "So nice."

"Come on, Wren." I tried to grab her hands across the table, but she pulled away from me, curling herself up in her chair and wrapping her arms around her knees.

"Won't work," she said.

"Will work. I'll be galloping through the woods and you'll be free like a bird."

"Most bird behavior is hardwired. Anyway, we'll get caught. Remember when you thought people would pay more money at our lemonade stand if we sold it in Mom's good crystal?"

"I was five."

"Or when you charged the neighborhood kids to see the invisible circus? Or, how about the time you talked me into helping you double all the numbers on the price tags in the store, then ran a half-price sale?"

"That happened to have been a great idea. My only mistake was telling Dad." I snorted. "Mr. Honesty."

"Yeah, yeah. And where are you going to tell Mr. Honesty you are every morning?" Wren asked.

"I don't know yet," I admitted. "But I'll come up with something. Maybe I can tell him that I joined the girls' softball league and that it practices in the morning."

"Is there a girls' softball league?"

"There must be."

"Alone in the tree house," Wren said dreamily. "That would be heaven on a stick."

"No. Riding every morning for a month. That's heaven."

Chapter 5

The sun was slipping below the horizon when I got home. I could tell immediately that something was wrong. My mother, dressed in a bathrobe and one fuzzy slipper, was pacing back and forth in the living area. Because the trailer was so small, she looked like she was actually bouncing off the walls.

"Hi, Mom." I tried to kiss her, but she whizzed by. "So, what's going on?"

Mom was so upset that she didn't even remind me to curtsy. "My amulet is flashing."

"Oh no," I said, flinging my hand across my forehead.

"Don't patronize the Magnificent Presence,

young lady. It is serious. It means that the Maluxzi-ads are here."

"Right here in the trailer?" I said. "Did you tell them it was too small for houseguests?"

According to my mother, the Maluxziads are an alien race who had taken over the planet Pannadeau, killing everyone in the royal family except for her. It was only due to her faithful servants that she was able to escape in the Imperial Pod. She was supposed to wind up on the planet Arishone with the rest of her people, but a wormhole opened up and she was sucked in, miraculously splashing down on Earth. Her pod sunk on impact and the wormhole, which was unstable, closed, so she's been living on our planet ever since. That's her story, and she sticks to it.

"I'm not kidding," my mother said in a tense voice.

"I know, Mom. I'm sorry." And I was sorry. Sorry that my mother was so crazy, and sorry I had to deal with it. "Did you get dressed today?" I asked. "Or eat anything?"

"On the radio I heard that dozens of people called the police about mysterious lights in the sky that looked like fireworks."

"Probably were fireworks."

"They were soundless and formed symbols like hieroglyphics." Mom began to pace again. "We've got to make a plan. A serious plan."

"And we will, Mom," I said, making my voice sound more patient than I felt. "Dad is taking Chuck to Pierce's baseball game, so it will be just you and me for dinner. How about you take a shower and get dressed? I'll make us a nice bowl of soup and a couple of sandwiches. Then, after you get dressed and eat something, we'll discuss it."

"Before the Maluxziads are ready to begin the attack, they have to find one another," Mom said.

"After your shower." I led Mom to the bathroom.

"That's probably what the fireworks were for. You know, to pinpoint their location."

"Come on, Mom." I turned the shower on and checked the water temperature. "We'll figure it out after dinner."

"Okay," Mom said a little more calmly. "Your father will be here at six-thirty to get Charles."

"Chuck's here?"

"In his room," Mom said.

I closed the bathroom door behind her, then ran through the tiny living space and threw open the door to the room I share with my brother. "Chuck. Chuck!"

There was no answer.

"Chuck, honey. It's me, Gracie." The tiny room was still. "Come out, come out wherever you are," I sang.

I opened the door to our closet and looked in. Nothing. "Chuck." I looked under the bottom bunk bed. There was a pillow wedged beneath it, and I could see one little shoe sticking out. "The lion drinks deep from the stream," I said.

"While the tiger sleeps beside the tree," Chuck whispered. It was our personal code. My mother insisted we have one in case of attack.

"It's me," I said. I pulled away the pillow. Chuck was lying curled up behind it. "Really me."

Chuck crawled out from under the bed. "Mom said the Maluxziads were here, so I was hiding. They want me 'cause I'm the next king, you know."

"Chuck," I said, patting his back. "Listen to me. We're not from Pannadeau. There are no Maluxziads."

"Yes, there are. They're weird-looking fish creatures the size of your thumb. But on Earth, they get inside plastic suits full of water and disguise themselves as humans and other animals. Then they get you. That's why I have to hide."

"Doesn't Mom, an alien, look exactly like other mothers here on Earth?"

"She's prettier," Chuck said loyally.

"Don't you and I look like all the other kids?"

"That's because our galaxy was seeded with the same stock," Chuck said. "Mom says it's like planting the same kind of wheat in different fields."

"I'm going to tell you a secret now. And you can't tell anyone. Do you promise?"

Chuck sat up and nodded his head solemnly.

"Mom and Dad met at a mental hospital called Barking Tree. Dad used to do odd handyman jobs for them when Mom was a patient."

"She's still patient."

"Patient like doctor and patient. She was a patient at Barking Tree because she talked about a make-believe place called Pannadeau."

"Pannadeau's not make-believe."

"Well, let's say it's like a special dream then. Mom's special dream."

Chuck crossed his arms over his chest. "Pannadeau's a real place. And if you don't stop telling lies, I'm going to have you locked in the dragon."

"Dungeon."

"Because I'm the next king and you're only a princess."

It was like trying to sell antiques to the penniless. "Okay. We'll talk about it later. How about you go wash your hands? Then I'll fix you a little snack before Dad picks you up for the game."

"Okay." Chuck walked into the kitchen, pausing to give an imaginary enemy a good karate chop in the kneecap. "Take that, you stupid Maluxziad," I heard him say.

Shaking my head, I opened the door to my parents' room. I could barely get in because Mom hadn't closed up the convertible bed. I fixed the blankets, then folded the bed back into a couch before going into the kitchen.

Mom hadn't done the dishes or cleared the table since breakfast. I gave Chuck a snack, then quickly put the tiny kitchen/living area back to rights. Everything was neat and normal-looking when Dad came home to pick up Chuck.

I didn't say anything to Dad about Mom's crazy behavior. He was looking forward to taking Chuck to see Pierce play, and I didn't want to upset him. Anyway, saying something meant having to do something about it.

"I got the information from the spy network," Mom said, pointing her head toward our portable radio.

"What do they do? Broadcast on WGBS in between the oldies?"

It was about a half hour later and Chuck and my father had gone. Mom sat across the table from me stirring what was left of her tomato soup and finishing up a chicken salad sandwich. She was freshly showered and would have looked normal if it weren't for her outfit, a tight black cat suit that looked like it was made out of rubber. She told me it was her fighting ensemble. I can only be thankful she didn't wear it on open school night.

"According to my informant," Mom said, "to

find one another the Maluxziads will say, 'Who will be brave enough to ride the horse of a different color?'"

"What do you mean, Wonder Woman?"

"Don't be sarcastic, Daughter. Listen." Mom leaned across the table and spoke earnestly. "On this planet the Maluxziads have to disguise their horrible selves in suits of water. If you see them, you must prick them as hard as you can. Remember, if you prick them hard enough, they will explode like giant water balloons and their internal fish creatures will die and disappear."

"Uh-huh."

"They can't survive without their suits." Mom took a folded piece of paper out of a white envelope, tipping it so that several necklaces fell into her hand. "That's why they wanted Pannadeau, you know," she said, her voice becoming gentle and dreamy. "An entire planet of gentle shallow seas with sprinkles of islands."

She sighed, then handed me one of the little necklaces. It was a thin chain with what looked like a long upside-down hat pin hanging from it. The pin ended with a white pearl. "Your very own Maluxziad pricker."

"Every girl should have at least one."

"A practical piece of jewelry that is equally at home on a coronation gown or a football jersey."

I turned it over in my hands. It happened to be quite pretty. "Where did you get it?"

"It came in the mail," Mom said, taking the last bite out of her sandwich.

"From Pannadeau? Like through the Intergalactic Express?"

"I think my best operative is here on Earth. Look." She pulled out a white piece of paper. It read: "A prick in time saves nine. Love, Nanny Goldstein."

"Nanny Goldstein?"

Mom put her finger over her lips, looked around the room, and motioned me closer. Cupping her hands around her mouth, she whispered into my ear. "That's not her real name."

"No kidding."

"It's Lady Vestia Dumare," she mouthed.

"What?"

She wrote the name down on the note.

"Vest—" I started to say.

"Shhh!" she said sharply, tearing the note into tiny pieces. She started whispering into my ear again. "When I was a little younger than you, this great lady managed to gain the confidence of the Maluxziads. In time, she became a high-level secret agent for Pannadeau. She must have come to Earth on the Maluxziad vessel."

I'm usually quick with a snappy comeback, but what my mother was saying was so off-the-wall that I was simply struck dumb.

"Even though the Maluxziads won the war," Mom said in her regular speaking voice, "I'm a loose end, unfinished business. And the Maluxziads are known for hating loose ends."

"Mmm-hmm."

"Don't patronize the Magnificent Presence, young lady. You and Charles are the true heirs of Pannadeau. That means you are loose ends, too, big ones." She dropped her voice. "And your lives are in danger."

She held up the Maluxziad pricker. "Now watch me." In one smooth motion, Mom grabbed the pearl and pulled out the pin. It was about an

62

inch and a half long and very sharp-looking. "In order to get the pin off, you have to squeeze the pearl. To put it back you squeeze it again and slip it into its sheath until you hear a little click."

Mom took one of the necklaces and put it around my neck. "Very nice," she said. "Now try to unsheathe it."

I tried but nothing happened.

"When you squeeze it, you should feel a little release. Then pull."

It took me a couple of tries to get the hang of it, but once I got it, I could do it every time.

"Now you are going to practice stabbing the chair," Mom said.

"Why? Is it an evil alien chair? Is it about to shuck off its pillow and attack us?"

"No. But it's old and shabby and we can't hurt it," she said mildly.

"I'll stab the chair if you want, but only under one condition."

"No conditions. This is a life-or-death situation." Mom got up from the table and began pacing back and forth. "I really must insist on your cooperation."

"My condition is that I want you to stop involving Chuck."

"It's my duty to warn him, same as you."

"When I came home Chuck was hiding under the bed because he thinks the Maluxziads are out to get him."

"Hiding is an important skill."

"He's only a little boy. And it's just not right to involve him in your fantasy world."

"Fantasy world!" She almost spit out the words. "How dare you!"

"How dare I? You're dressed in a fighting outfit!" I yelled.

"Fighting ensemble," she corrected.

"And if you don't cut it out, you're going to wind up back at Barking Tree. Is that what you want to happen?"

"Why would I possibly go back to Barking Tree?"

"Because it's a mental institution. And you're . . ." I couldn't finish the rest of the sentence.

"Gracie. Darling. I wasn't at Barking Tree because I was crazy. My mental instability was just a cover story. I was at Barking Tree because I lost my amulet when my pod crashed into the lake on the Barking Tree property. I also needed a quiet place to get the lay of the land, get used to Earth's gravity, and get into good physical shape. You know, your father was the one who found it."

"Found what?"

"My amulet. It had fallen into the satellite dish. Last place I would have looked. But your father was always so intelligent." She smiled, remembering.

Taking a deep breath, I said, "Listen to me, Mom. Chuck's five, too young to defend himself, anyway. Plus, there is always an adult with him, usually you, me, or Dad. No Maluxziad can get past us." I looked Mom square in the eyes. "I promise."

"He's still the future king. Not that there's a kingdom anymore."

"Here's the deal. If you don't stop talking to Chuck about the Maluxziads, I will refuse to learn how to fight them. But if you agree to say nothing to Chuck, I will practice whatever it is you want me to learn."

I crossed my arms and leaned back on the chair. Mom looked at me and I stared right back at her. After a moment she sighed. "You are as stubborn as your grandfather, the great King Leon." Finally she nodded her head. "All right."

"All right, what?"

"Charles won't be told what's going on until he's older. Now watch." In a fluid motion, Mom removed her Maluxziad pricker, leaped from her chair, and crouched into a fighting position. With lightning speed, she threw her arm out, making a quick motion. "Front stab."

She leaped to the right, stretching her arm so that it was at a right angle. "Side stab." She whipped around in a fluid motion, spinning on her left foot and lifting her right leg up high. "Back gambit with kick."

I stared at my mother. "Wow. You're a regular fighting machine."

Mom clicked the Maluxziad pricker back into her necklace and brushed her hands together. "It's like riding a water cycle. Now it's your turn."

"Do I get a fighting ensemble?"

"Have you earned a fighting ensemble? Now get up."

Feeling like a jerk, I pulled out my pricker and pierced the chair in the corner.

"Not bad for the first time. And remember. They steal their brains, so don't strike them in the head."

I decided to let that one pass. "Okay," I said.

"Now stab the chair again."

As I attempted to spear the chair, Mom kept up a patter of encouragement. "And lift. And strike. Good. And lift and strike and lift and strike," she said rhythmically. She sounded like an instructor on a television exercise show. "Hold your arm steady. Good. And again."

I flailed away at the chair, lifting my arm and striking in the prescribed manner. If it wasn't such a totally nutso thing to be doing, it would almost have been fun.

"Excellent, Daughter. You're a natural."

"Thank you," I said, panting.

"If you hear someone say, 'Who will be brave enough to ride the horse of a different color?' you stab him, good and hard. It's important because the Maluxziads' water weapons are very powerful."

"Water weapons?"

"That's right. The new Niagara Eight can blow a person a hundred feet. So you must stab first and think later. Got that?"

I didn't say anything.

"Gracie," she said sharply.

"It's just so ridiculous."

"It may be ridiculous, but it's still their code. Promise me."

Who was going to say something like that to me, anyway? "Okay," I agreed.

"Swear it."

"I swear."

"Good. Now I want you to practice for a half hour a night and you have to promise me to always wear your Maluxziad pricker."

"I promise."

"And protect Chuck."

"I will always protect Chuck," I said sincerely.

And that's how, two weeks later, I was standing down by the estate gates waiting for a limousine to take me to Camp Greenlong, wearing Wren's summer castoffs and my Maluxziad pricker.

CHAPTER 6

Dad tells me that the early bird catches the worm. But in my experience it mostly stands around, getting more and more nervous, while it waits for the rest of the flock to show up.

It was 8:25 in the morning, and I had been standing at the gate for more than a half hour waiting for Wren to appear. She was going to confirm that all systems were go, give me any last minute information I might need, and make sure I got off, before retreating to the tree house.

Finally, I heard her front door slam. I relaxed, then tensed up again when I heard the sound of a car engine starting. A minute later Wren and her mother drove down the driveway. This was definitely not in the game plan.

Aunt Leora stuck her head out of the car window. "Good morning, Gracie," she said. "Glorious day."

"Just taking a walk," I blurted out.

Wren hopped out of the car looking extremely grumpy.

"You have your water bottle, bathing suit, and flip-flops?" Aunt Leora asked Wren.

"Yes, Mom," Wren said, patting her knapsack. She turned her back on her mother and mouthed, "What are we going to do?"

I shrugged my shoulders.

"I see you're wearing the French shorts Wren grew out of, and carrying her old knapsack, too," Aunt Leora said to me as she got out of the car. "You look very nice."

"Just taking a walk," I repeated.

Aunt Leora glanced at her watch and pursed her lips. "He's late. I knew it was too good to be true when the limo company called to offer such a low price." She looked critically at Wren, who was twirling her hair like crazy. "I bought you a beautiful ChicSwim."

"Thank you," Wren said politely.

"You don't even know that a ChicSwim is a bathing suit, do you? For goodness' sakes, it's in all the fashion magazines."

"I read science magazines," Wren said.

"How are you going to learn anything that way?" Aunt Leora sighed.

A black limousine pulled into the gates and my aunt waved the driver over. I grabbed Wren's hand. "You've got to get rid of your mother," I whispered.

"I know," she whispered back. "Hey, Mom," she called out. "I'm suddenly feeling very nervous. Would you do me a favor and not see me off?"

Aunt Leora patted her shoulder. "Since there was a little mix-up about time, I want to introduce myself to the driver and make sure that he knows who you are and where you're going and all that."

A blond young man who didn't look a day older than eighteen got out of the limousine. He introduced himself as Lance Lyway and apologized for being late, saying that he was new to the area and had gotten lost. When Aunt Leora asked him where he was from, he paused, then finally said Norway. I sure hoped he knew the way to Camp Greenlong.

"We need a plan," Wren whispered.

"We need a miracle," I said gloomily. Thinking furiously, I rocked back and forth on the balls of my feet. Suddenly, I got it. "The driver doesn't know which one of us is you. Let's keep it that way. Then we'll both get into the car and you'll get out at the corner, okay?"

Wren bit her lip and nodded. "Okay."

Aunt Leora turned to us. "Lance, this is my daughter, Wren Baldwin," she said.

"Wave now," I said, trying to speak without moving my lips. Wren and I stood next to each other and waved in unison.

"Starting tomorrow, Lance will pick you up at eight o'clock, then retrieve you at one." She walked over to Wren and pecked the air.

I leaned over and gave Aunt Leora an air kiss, too. I don't know whether or not it had any effect on the driver, but it sure confused my aunt.

Lance opened the back door and Wren got into

the car. Before he could shut it, I bounded in behind her.

Aunt Leora raised her eyebrows. "Where do you think you're going, young lady?"

"Just to the highway," Wren said.

"That's right," I agreed quickly.

"That way it will be easier to get to the shop," Wren said.

"Working at the shop," I said.

Crossing her arms across her chest, Aunt Leora said, "All right. Just for today I'll allow it. But, I don't want this to be a regular thing. Is that clear?"

"Like a bell," I said.

As soon as the car was rolling, I said, "Mothers!" in my loudest voice. Wren and I gave each other a high five. When the driver rounded the corner, Wren told him to stop.

"Hey," Lance said. "I thought I was taking you to Camp Greenlong."

"You're taking me," I said.

"You're Wren Baldwin?"

"That's right."

"I'm Gracie Quicksilver Wright, her cousin," Wren said.

Lance smiled at Wren. "Gracie Quicksilver Wright. Well, hi," he said, turning around in his seat. "You know I don't really mind dropping you off at whatever store you are going to."

I took a closer look at him. He was extraordinarily handsome.

"That's real nice of you," Wren said. "But I forgot my . . ." She paused.

"Toothbrush," I said as Wren rolled her eyes.

"Really," Lance said, smiling. "It would be my pleasure."

"No, it's okay." Wren looked down and her cheeks burned a bright shade of pink.

The limousine pulled to a stop. "One-thirty, tree house," I said.

"One-thirty," Wren agreed. "Bye, Lance," she said, reaching over to open the car door.

"No, let me." Lance leaped out of the car. He ran around the limousine like he was practicing for the marathon and opened the door with a flourish. "There you go," he said.

"Thanks," Wren whispered.

"Bye, Gracie." Lance stood for moment looking at her.

Wren turned around and waved.

"Hel-LO," I called from inside the car.

Lance opened the door, got back into the limousine, and we pulled away.

"This is so great," I said to Lance. "Nice and roomy." I lay down in the backseat, then hopped up. "So," I said, "how do you like driving a limousine?"

Lance touched a button in his front console, and the window between us went up.

"And I bet the best part is getting to know the passengers, huh?" I said to the glass.

About twenty minutes later, we passed a sign that said GREENLONG ESTATES AND NATURE PRESERVE: HOME OF CAMP GREENLONG. Lance drove through the gates and down a long road. We passed through a topiary archway that opened up into a huge meadow surrounded by fields and dotted with cabins. Lance dropped me off by the side of a small blue cottage. A sign under the window said ADMINIS-TRATION OFFICE.

"This is it," Lance said, lowering the window between us slightly. I waited for Lance to open the door for me the way he did for my cousin. He didn't move.

"It's the leprosy, isn't it?" I said. Feeling silly, I opened the door and got out. Practically before I hit the dirt, Lance drove off.

Swallowing hard, I looked at the blue building. All at once, my stomach tightened. There was no going back now.

CHAPTER 7

Through the open window of the administration office, a woman's voice bellowed, "Just waiting for the last of the little snots to show up."

I knocked on the door. A tall, big-shouldered woman just on this side of fat threw it open. She had a square face and short brown hair streaked with gray. "You are?" she boomed.

"Wren Baldwin. The last of the little snots," I said.

"I'm Lady Gregson," she said, extending a meaty hand. "A big, fat, enormous snot." She gave me a handshake hearty enough to knock apples out of a tree. I noticed that her hand was rough and her nails were short and polish-free.

"You don't look like the daughter of a duke and a princess," I said.

Lady Gregson was wearing a dress covered by a full-length, earth-covered apron. Sharp-looking gardening tools stuck out of enormous pockets bulging with seed catalogs, bags of fertilizer, and what could have been a jar of worms. "I'm from the eccentric branch of the family."

I nodded. I knew what that was like.

"Come in," Lady Gregson said, grabbing my arm and pulling me into her office. The room didn't go with her at all. The walls were eggshell blue and covered with small, delicate watercolors. The furniture was made of a lacy white wicker, and there were vases of artistically arranged flowers scattered about.

A policewoman with a nose that could rival Pinocchio's was pacing around the office. She took one look at me and began hitting her thigh with a nightstick she took out of her belt. The nightstick made a sharp sound. *Slap. Slap. Slap.*

It was a good thing I couldn't get any more

nervous or I would have had a heart attack on the spot.

"This is our local bobby, Officer Sharpe," Lady Gregson said. "She's here investigating some vandalism. Last night some kids broke into the camp grounds and spray-painted graffiti on the barn roof."

"No kidding," I said.

"No kidding," Officer Sharpe said. She tapped her broomstick of a nose. "Trouble makes my nose twitch. And it's been twitching since you walked in the door."

"Maybe you need an antihistamine," I said.

"Maybe you need a night in the pokey," she said to me.

"Maybe you should finish your investigations," Lady Gregson said to Officer Sharpe.

Officer Sharpe walked to the door and pulled it open. "I'll be keeping an eye on you," she said to me. She slapped her nightstick smartly against her leg as she walked out.

"Come on," Lady Gregson said, checking her watch. "The other kids in your riding group should be getting down to the stable."

"Great. I've never ridden before and I'm really looking forward to it," I said.

Lady Gregson looked down at a four-by-five card with Wren's name on it, then back at me. "Really? Your mother said that you were afraid of horses."

Whoops. "Oh yeah. A little," I covered. "But I love horses." I paused. "Even though they're a little scary." I sounded like an idiot.

"Well, I'll show you where to change and put your stuff. Then I'll take you down to the stable."

On the way to my cabin, Lady Gregson told me a little about the camp, which backed into Greenlong Estates and Nature Preserve. "It's the largest tract of undeveloped land in the county," she said, looking around proudly.

"It is beautiful," I agreed. Lady Gregson gave me my schedule. In the morning, I had riding and horsemanship with the beginners' group. For an elective, I could sign up for anything I chose. But if I wanted to take sailing, canoeing, or water skiing, I had to pass the deep-water test.

"No problem," I said. I was an ace swimmer.

"So your fear of water hasn't kept you from swimming?" Lady Gregson asked.

I resolved to stop speaking altogether. "Just bathing," I joked.

I put my stuff away in a locker with Wren's name on it. Lady Gregson led me out of my cabin, through a trail in the woods, then down a grassy hill to the meadow where the stable was located. She trotted along, moving swiftly for a woman of her size and bulk.

The riding area consisted of a big barn attached to a large indoor ring and several smaller outbuildings. There was a big grassy paddock on one side, and two outdoor riding rings, one bigger than the other. A group of workmen were repainting the graffiti on the barn roof, which looked almost like hieroglyphics.

Lady Gregson shaded her eyes with her hand as a thin old man with chin-length white hair and a face so wrinkled it could double as a waffle came over to us. "Stedman," Lady Gregson called. "This is the one we talked about. Wren Baldwin."

"Hey now, Wren," he said. His voice was gravelly but gentle and soothing. "I'm Tom Stedman, and this here is my grandson Hart, who will be helping me out this summer." He gestured to a long-limbed, auburn-haired boy who looked about fifteen. Hart gave me a friendly wave. He was holding a big light-colored bay. Behind Hart, on his other side, was a pinto.

The big bay stood perfectly still. "That wild thing that Hart is hanging on to for dear life is Stout, who you'll be riding this summer," Stedman said, breaking into a grin.

Stout stood motionless. Not even his tail twitched.

"I understand that you've never ridden before," Stedman continued. "You'll like Stout. He's as gentle as a lamb."

Stout looked gentle all right. In fact, he looked like he was asleep. Maybe dead.

"Hi, Stout," I said. The horse didn't move a muscle.

"Here, try a little treat." Stedman took a piece of carrot out of his breast pocket and handed it to me. "Put it on your palm and hold your hand perfectly straight," he said. "Now reach out and put it under Stout's nose."

I did. After a minute Stout put his nose into my palm. I could feel the gentle breeze from his nostrils. He opened his lips and scooped up the carrot.

"All right, Stout," I said, patting his neck. "What a horse."

The pinto on the other side of Hart put his head on Hart's head and stared at me.

"Who's that one? With the soulful eyes."

Hart grinned. "She thinks you're soulful, girl." He reached up to stroke the pinto's neck.

"That's Hart's special horse, Dog," Stedman said.

"Dog?"

"Because of the way she follows him around," Stedman said.

"Wren," Lady Gregson called. "There's a girl in your group who says that you guys are friends."

"What?" I screeched, spinning around.

Coming out of the stable leading a gray horse was a girl with shiny brown hair and a nose that was not made by God. I recognized her by her evil grin. It was the girl at Wren's birthday dinner— Ann Armstrong.

CHAPTER 8

I closed my eyes and willed myself to disappear in a puff of smoke. But when I opened them again, I was still at Camp Greenlong and Ann was still coming at me. Any minute she would open her mouth, and Wren and I would be sentenced to long, boring lectures from our parental units that would probably go on until Wren's parents moved into the Hole in One Nursing Home and Golf Village and mine moved into the trailer behind it.

"Hello"—she paused for one long second—"Wren."

"What?" I yelped.

"Wren, Wren, Wren. Well." Ann put on a big

phony smile and turned to Lady Gregson. "Wren and I are cocaptains of the junior cheerleading squad at Whitmore."

I was pretty sure she wasn't helping me out for humanitarian reasons. Still, I had no choice but to go along. "Right," I said, trying to smile. "Cheerleading. Uh, sis boom . . ."

"Bah." Ann raised her fist in the air, causing her horse to startle and rear back.

"She scares the football players even worse," I said.

Hart let out a brief snort of laughter, but Ann glared at me. "Watch it"—she paused—"Wren."

"Helps them play really well," I said.

Two boys, each with a horse in tow, joined our group. They were in the middle of a heated discussion. The smaller of the two, who wore large tortoiseshell glasses and had a face like a monkey, was talking. "Statistically, it's not possible that we're the only culture in the universe. I mean we're dealing with infinite numbers here," he said.

"You Americans always forget, how you say, time variable," the other boy said in what could have been a Russian accent. He was huge, with a football player's physique, and his wary, close-set eyes made him look older, too. He leaned down to flick some dirt off his brand-new jodphurs. I suddenly noticed that everyone except me was wearing an expensive riding outfit.

"You kids need to pay attention to Stedman now," Lady Gregson said. "You can talk later."

"Thank you, Lady Gregson," Ann said, putting her arm around my shoulders. "Wren and I have so much to talk about."

"Like my funeral," I muttered, pulling away.

"Love that topic," Ann said sweetly.

After Lady Gregson left, Stedman took over. He explained the parts of the bridle and showed us how to get a bit into a horse's mouth.

"Can we ride now?" Ann asked when he finished.

"First, I want to see you bridle your horse," Stedman said.

"Can't stable boy over there do it?" asked Ann, tilting her head to Hart.

Hart stiffened.

"His name is Hart Stedman," Stedman said

calmly. "And no, he can't. The object of the program here at Greenlong is to turn you kids into horsemen and horsewomen. To do that you have to know how to take complete care of your mount."

Ann wrinkled up her nose. "Can't I just do the riding part?"

"Sorry," Stedman said. "If you want to stay in this program, you must participate in all of it. That means plenty of riding, sure, but it also means knowing how to bridle, saddle, groom, and feed your horse. Even muck out its stall."

"You want me to touch horse doody?"

"Why don't you eat it?" Hart muttered to himself.

I covered my mouth with my hands to hide a smile.

"If you do not want to participate in the riding program, you don't have to," Stedman said to Ann. "You can still swim and sail and play tennis. Should I tell Lady Gregson that you're dropping out?"

"No," Ann said sullenly.

"Okay," Stedman said, turning to me. "So, Wren, are you ready to bridle up Stout?"

I had so much on my mind that I hadn't been paying close enough attention to the actual bridling. "I, uh." I shook my head no.

"Another prima donna?" he said in an annoyed voice.

"No, no. It's not that. I mean I just—uh—I was—uh . . ."

"I'm sorry. I forgot," Stedman said kindly. "Stout's the gentlest horse in the world. Here, let me show you and everyone else again."

This time I watched carefully. And I was able to get the bit into Stout's mouth on my first try.

"See how good it feels to face your fears," Stedman said.

"Mmm-hmm," I murmured. Aunt Leora must have given the camp a real earful.

After the two boys got their horses bridled, it was Ann's turn again. She flubbed her first two attempts to get the bit into her horse's mouth. "Open your mouth, you stupid animal," Ann said in an annoyed voice.

"That's right. Charm him into it," I said.

Ann gave me a look that could french a fry.

"Nice riding clothes. You get them at one of the many garage sales you frequent?"

"Pay attention to Patter, Ann," Stedman said. "Here, let me help you." Together they got the bit into Patter's mouth. "Good job. Now come, bring your horses over next to the ring."

As soon as Stedman was out of earshot, Ann started. "Wren has an aunt who thinks she's an alien," she announced.

"Really?" the smaller boy said excitedly. "I've been studying UFO sightings for years. I'm particularly interested in animal mutilations and crop circles."

"That's fascinating, Vernon," Ann drawled in a voice that clearly indicated it wasn't.

Vernon didn't seem to notice, though. "It is, isn't it?" he said enthusiastically. "Just a month ago, two goats were found with their brains removed. Right here on Lady Gregson's property."

"Hey. I heard about that," I said.

"And before that," Vernon continued, "two people turned up dead without brains. It's certainly not a coincidence."

The large boy with the accent spoke up. "Not coincidence. Not aliens. Robbery criminals."

"Come on, Kip. They were stitched up with teeny-tiny stitches. Definitely not made by humans," Vernon said. "Plus lots of locals reported seeing weird lights in the sky, like fireworks."

"Believing in aliens is most ignorant," Kip said firmly.

"Maybe not ignorant," I said. "Maybe just misguided."

"No, he's right. People who believe in aliens are stupid," Ann said. "But not as stupid as people who actually believe they are aliens."

I clutched Stout's reins so tightly my knuckles turned white.

"Though mostly they're crazy," Ann continued.

I took a step toward her. "Watch what you say about people's relatives," I hissed.

"Now, now. It's not like we're talking about your mother or anything," Ann said. "Right"—she paused—"Wren?"

"You should keep an open mind, Ann," Vernon said. "If you want, I'll show you a file of evidence that conclusively proves aliens exist."

"No thanks."

"They say opposites attract, you know," Vernon said, pushing his glasses back up his nose and giving Ann a toothy smile.

"Make the heart grow fonder, yes?" Kip said.

"That's absence," Ann said to Kip, while glaring at Vernon.

"I love the American idiom," Kip said.

"Come closer, guys," Stedman called. I looked up and saw that Stedman was in the middle of the riding ring. Hart was on Dog. We led our horses over to the ring.

While Stedman explained the difference between the gaits, Hart demonstrated, showing us the correct body positions riders use to walk, trot, canter, and gallop.

Hart rode so smoothly it was like he was a part of the horse. He ended the demonstration by doing a handstand on his saddle, then jumping off Dog, landing neatly on his feet. He took a bow. Dog did, too, and we all applauded.

"Wow," I said to him. "You could be a circus performer or an animal trainer."

"I want to go to veterinary school."

"No kidding. That's great," I burbled. "I wish I could ride like that."

Hart grinned. "All it takes is practice," he said cheerfully.

Hart hopped over the fence and helped me mount up. "Thanks," I said, smiling down at him happily. "It's cool being up this high."

"Yeah, I like that part, too," Hart said, grinning back at me. "Hold your reins right. Like this," he said, arranging my hands in the proper position. When he touched me, a little tingle shot through my hands and into my heart. "Perfect."

I must have had a stupid grin on my face, because Ann was on me like a dealer at the flea market.

"Don't get too friendly," Ann said in a loud whisper. "You know your mother would collapse if her precious darling, one of the department store Baldwins, got a crush on a common stable boy."

"Who said anything about a crush?" I whispered back a little too loudly.

"Hey," Hart said to me. "The common stable boy has excellent hearing. Also, he doesn't date rich snobs."

"I, uh, I didn't say—I didn't mean—I wouldn't . . ." My voice trailed off.

Hart gave me a fake smile. "So you can relax now, Princess."

"I am not a princess," I snapped.

"She is, on her high horse, yes?" Kip said.

After we were all mounted and were holding the reins properly, Stedman had us walk our horses in a big circle. "Okay, kids, back straight, eyes front, heels down, elbows in. Shorten your reins a little, Ann. No, not that much. Relax, Kip. Lasso isn't going to hurt you. Toes up, Vernon. Excellent, Wren."

Hart was outside the ring riding a red horse in a circle while Dog watched. Stedman told us that the red horse was named Cinnamon, that she had been abused and that he and Hart were trying to help her. Cinnamon, who was considered too difficult for the campers to ride, reared up, and Hart spoke softly to her.

Although I couldn't help sneaking the occasional peek at Hart, I concentrated on my own mount, enjoying the solid feel of Stout beneath me and the delicious aroma of horse that wafted off his great neck. I felt deeply and utterly at home.

But, as soon as I got off Stout, Ann made a bee-line for me. "Let's walk to the cabin together, then we can change for swimming." She grabbed my hand and started pulling me along.

I broke away. "Let go. We're not actually engaged."

"No," Ann said nastily. "Our relationship is going to be better than that. More like master and slave, I think."

We walked in silence for a moment. "So," I said when I could wait no longer. "What exactly do you want?"

"Well, slave, I have to write a history paper over the summer. Somebody does, anyway," she said, lifting up her eyebrows and winking.

"You sure don't want me to write it. I maintain a gentlewoman's C myself," I said.

"You mean a trailer-trash C, don't you?" Ann said in a nasty voice.

My face burned.

"Well, if you don't want to get into big trouble, you can write an A paper this summer," Ann said.

"And if I won't?"

We walked by the canoe shack where Lady Gregson was trimming some flowers. "If you don't deadhead them, they don't keep blooming," she announced to no one.

"Oh, Lady Gregson," Ann said. "Remember this morning you were talking about doing a talent show? Wren is a great piano player. What did you say you were working on, Wren?"

"Uh, Mozart's Eleventh," I mumbled.

"The Concerto in F or the Symphony in D?" Lady Gregson asked.

"Huh?"

"She could play it in the talent show," Ann said cheerfully.

"I, uh, don't think . . . ," I stumbled.

"We'd love to have you perform, Wren," Lady Gregson said.

"My paper is on the history of anything," Ann said after we had passed her. "Six pages. Typed."

When I got home, I immediately dashed to the tree house. Wren was there, smiling to herself and working on a sketch.

"What are you drawing?" I asked, climbing up.

"Bluebird," Wren said, quickly closing the sketch pad. She moved so fast that I only managed a quick peek. Still, her bluebird looked remarkably like Lance, the handsome limousine driver.

"Must be the bluebird of happiness," I said slyly.

Then my cousin, who never talked about males at all, except for stuff like the mating rituals of the frigate bird—which, for those who are interested, puffs up a red pouch on his chest to attract females during the breeding season—abruptly changed the subject. "So tell me," she said quickly, "how did it go?"

I filled my cousin in on what had happened. "I don't think Ann wants to rat us out," I concluded. "She just wants power."

"That and a paper," Wren said, nervously twirling her hair. "Not that I wouldn't enjoy writing it."

My cousin was probably the only person in America who liked being blackmailed into schoolwork.

"Just don't make it too good," I said. Like she could help herself.

"I've always been interested in the Peloponnesian War."

Knowing that if I let her go on I'd have to hear about the battle of Peloponnesia or something, I cut Wren off. "After a certain point, if Ann told on us, she'd get in trouble, too. Her mother and the camp would want to know why she knew something so important about us and didn't let on. Might give us something to dangle over her head."

"Well, it's no Sword of Damocles," Wren said.

"Indeed."

CHAPTER 9

After a couple of days, I had a routine. As soon as Lance dropped me off at camp, I'd run down to Big Paddock, the grassy enclosure next to the stables. I'd sit on the fence and admire Shimmer, the camp's beautiful brand-new filly.

I'd sit there dreaming about maybe owning a horse someday until Lady Gregson signaled the morning meeting. "Coo-ee!" she'd holler, sounding more like a pig farmer than the lady of the manor.

Once the kids were assembled on Square Green, Lady Gregson presided over the raising of the flag and announcements. After morning meeting was horsemanship and riding, followed by a snack, Lady Gregson called elevenses, then free choice until Lance picked me up at one o'clock.

One morning I was leaning against the fence of Big Paddock cooing at Shimmer when I heard, "Thrust, parry, advance, hit. Yes, a hit!"

I peered around the corner. There, with his back to me, was Hart. He was holding a fencing sword and fighting with an imaginary opponent. I cleared my throat and Hart twirled around abruptly.

"What are you doing here?" he snapped.

I looked at Hart with his straight back and clear green eyes and felt a sudden need to sit down. "Watching you."

"Well, go away."

"So, you fence?" I said lamely.

"Duh."

"You don't have to be so snotty."

"Yeah. You and your friend Ann have that all sewed up."

"I've never been anything but nice to you. Never, ever. So don't blame me for Ann, who I can't stand, anyway."

"I thought you guys were good friends."

"Well, you thought wrong."

Hart absently played with his fencing foil, bending it up and down. "My dad used to fence."

"How come he stopped?"

"He died."

"Oh no," I said, squishing my eyes closed. "I'm so sorry."

"Not your fault."

"Really. I'm just stupid sometimes."

I think I looked so upset that Hart took pity on me. "There's no way you could have known," Hart said in a friendlier voice. "Anyway, my guidance counselor told me that good schools were always looking for kids for their fencing teams. I'll need a scholarship to pay for college."

"I know what that's like," I said.

"How? From books?"

"Can't you get a riding scholarship?" I asked, trying to cover.

"There are no colleges around here that offer anything like that. And I can't leave my grandfather. He's getting old and needs help. Not that he'll admit it. Anyway . . . ," he said, his voice trailing off. Hart lifted his foil and crouched down in a fencing pose. "*En garde,*" he said, lunging toward me.

"En garde yourself," I said, picking up a twig and wielding it like a sword.

"Parry, riposte, lunge," he yelled, dancing forward then back. His foil whipped through the air.

Holding the twig, I ran to his side, then, using a maneuver my mother taught me, pretended to stab him. "Side stab!" I yelled.

Dog whinnied and stepped forward. "It's okay, Dog," Hart said. "We were only playing." He threw an arm around Dog's neck. "She's protective," he said to me. "Anyway, there's no such thing as a side stab."

"You've obviously never been to Dorothea Wright's Training Academy for Maluxziad Warfare," I said.

"Huh?"

"Private joke." I was still working out with my mother every night. "So, I guess you win with your secret equine weapon, Dog, the wonder horse." I reached out to pat the pinto and smiled at Hart. We were about a foot apart and the air suddenly felt electric between us.

"Yeah. Well." Hart looked down and kicked the dirt. "See how the other half lives."

"What do you mean?"

"The half that doesn't have limousines bringing them to exclusive camps, that would have to work all week to take someone like you out for an evening, and has to think about scholarships and pocket money," he said harshly.

"I happen to work," I said.

"Yeah, right."

"I do. And I'd be happy to go to a diner and have a burger."

"Ha. Listen. I'm not allowed to be rude to the campers, and you're not supposed to be down here. And," he said, his voice rising, "unlike you so-called working girls and guys who pay for the experience of mucking out stalls and pretending to be horsemen, I have to do it for real."

"What are you getting so mad about all of a sudden?"

"I'm not mad!" he yelled.

Suddenly, Lady Gregson's voice blasted, her "coo-ee!" causing a wave of neighing and hoof stamping from the stable.

"All right."

"Better go, Princess," Hart said. "There's no limousine waiting, so you'll have to rough it up the hill yourself."

"I am not a princess!" I yelled. Then I turned and ran up the hill.

I couldn't believe how at home I felt on a horse after only a few lessons.

"Trot now," Stedman told the class.

"Come on, Stout," I said. I squeezed my legs around Stout's body and clicked my mouth. Stout broke into a slow trot.

"She's a real natural, she is," Stedman said to Hart.

Hart frowned at me.

"All right," Stedman said. "Wren," he called to me, "I want you to try something new. Keeping Stout at a trot, circle him around the edge of the ring, then bring him through the center and around in the other direction. It's like making a big figure eight."

I nudged Stout, then made a perfect figure eight in the center of the ring.

"Nice job," Stedman said.

After I dismounted, Stedman pulled me aside. "So, how would you feel about a new mount? One with a little more go."

"Okay," I said. "Sure."

"I was thinking about Flash."

"Flash!" I practically glowed with pleasure. Flash was a beautiful horse, all black except for a white stocking on his right foreleg and a matching star on his forehead. Unlike Stout, the challenge of riding Flash would be holding him back rather than keeping him going. "Really, really?"

"We'll start you tomorrow," Stedman said.

"Ooh, I'm so happy. Not that I won't always love you, Stout," I said, hugging the big bay.

After putting Stout back in his stall, I went to see Flash. He was housed across the aisle from the once abused Cinnamon, who had a hand-painted sign over her stall that said: DON'T TOUCH ME. I'M SHY AND DON'T LIKE PEOPLE. I was stroking Flash's silky nose when Ann came over to me.

"Well," she said nastily, "I see Stedman's favorite girl got the best horse in the stable."

"He is a beauty, isn't he?" I said dreamily.

"Hart told me he's a little wild."

"He did?" I said. My voice came out a little higher than usual, and Ann immediately picked up on it.

"Ooh. Someone likes Hart," she said.

"Cut it out, Ann."

"Little crush, have you?" she teased.

"I do not have a crush on Hart Stedman!" I yelled at Ann.

"I don't have a crush on you either!" Hart yelled from down the barn.

I turned around and banged the stall with my palm in frustration.

Flash, sensing a change in the atmosphere, reared back and whinnied.

I stepped back. "Sorry, horse," I said to Flash.

Ann snorted. "Different from your sleepy old bay. Well, we'll see tomorrow who will be brave enough to ride the horse of a different color," she said.

I spun around. Without thinking, I whipped out my Maluxziad pricker and stabbed her in the shoulder.

CHAPTER 10

Unfortunately, Ann didn't explode. Instead, she let out a scream loud enough to be heard in Hawaii. Holding on to her arm, she stared at the tiny drop of blood that stained her white shirt.

Moving with lightning speed, I slipped my Maluxziad pricker back into its holder around my neck. I heard it click in and sighed with relief. But when I looked up, Hart, who had come running to see what the scream was about, met my eyes.

Stedman ran over to Ann, followed by Vernon and Kip. "What happened?" Stedman asked.

"That little piece of no-good trailer trash stabbed me," Ann said.

"Watch who you call trailer trash," I yelled back.

"Cat fight. Cat fight," Vernon said.

"Where is cat?" Kip asked, lifting his massive shoulders.

"Ann, are you accusing Wren Baldwin of attacking you?" Stedman asked.

"She's really not Wren—"

"Remember the Peloponnesian War!" I yelled. I took a step forward, crossed my arms across my chest, and locked eyes with her.

"The cat is Peloponnesian, yes?" Kip said, sounding confused.

Ann opened her mouth.

"Six pages and every word brilliant," I said.

"Wren," Stedman said, "what do you have to say for yourself?"

Saying I stabbed her with my pricker because I thought she was a Maluxziad invader just wouldn't hack it. "Uh . . ."

I was saved from having to say anything, because at that very moment, Lady Gregson, carrying a large shovel and dressed in a long skirt, muddy boots, and a large hat, walked into the stable. "What's going on?" she asked.

"Wren stabbed Ann," Vernon said.

"Did not," I said.

"Show us your injury, Ann," Stedman said.

"She's not exactly gushing blood," Lady Gregson remarked.

A wasp landed on one of the flowers in Lady Gregson's hat. Suddenly I had an inspiration. "A bee was buzzing around her. I swatted it, that's all," I said.

"It doesn't look like a bee sting," Lady Gregson said. "More like a pinprick."

"Pinprick?" Kip said, his voice rising as he looked me up and down.

"Vernon, did you actually see Wren stab Ann?" Lady Gregson asked.

"No. But Ann said she did," he said, as if that settled the matter.

"Don't support me," Ann yelled at Vernon.

"But you did say so."

"Shut up," Ann said.

"Empty your pockets, Wren," Lady Gregson said.

I pulled out my keys, some money, and a comb and deposited them onto the tack table.

"Well, I don't see a weapon. Hart, I want you to escort everyone but Wren out of here."

"Yes, ma'am," Hart said. "Come on, everyone." He gestured at the rest of the group. Reluctantly, Kip, Ann, and Vernon followed him out of the stables.

Lady Gregson's dirt-stained hand played over her face while she looked at me. "So," she said softly when everyone had left. "Tell me."

"Well," I said, rocking back and forth and clasping my hands in front of my chest. "A bee landed on Ann's shoulder and must have stung her before I swatted it."

"I think I'm going to give your mother a call. Make sure you haven't made a habit of stabbing people in the past."

I sighed with relief. I knew my mother would support me completely.

Lady Gregson pulled a cell phone out of her pocket. "What's your number, Wren?"

Wren? I suddenly realized that Lady Gregson wasn't going to call my mother but Wren's mother. And I couldn't give her my mother's number, because my mother thought I was out playing softball.

I gave Lady Gregson the Baldwins' number and watched as she dialed. Blanca answered. She informed Lady Gregson that Mrs. Baldwin was playing golf but would return the call when she returned.

Hart came back in. As soon as Lady Gregson put the phone back in her pocket, he spoke. "I wanted to say that I saw it happen."

"What did you see?"

"I saw a bee flying around Ann and Wren swatting it."

"Why didn't you say anything before, Hart?" Stedman asked.

"None of my business."

"Then why say anything now?"

"Because Wren's got a lot of natural talent and I don't want to see her get kicked out of camp." With that, Hart turned and marched out of the stable.

"You believe that?" Lady Gregson asked Stedman.

Stedman's eyes turned steely. "My grandson doesn't lie, Lady Gregson."

"Wren, you can go to the waterfront now," Lady Gregson said.

"What are you going to tell my mother?" I asked.

"That you're adjusting well and having a wonderful time."

As soon as I got home, I ran directly to the tree house. Wren was just climbing down to go to her piano lesson. While I walked her home, I brought her up to speed on the day's adventures. So neither of us was too surprised when Aunt Leora ran out of the house beaming. "Lady Gregson says that you have a natural seat and are doing wonderfully. Not only that, she says you're swimming and boating. I knew you could do it if you tried."

Wren shot me a stricken look over her mother's shoulder.

"Oh. And she also told me something so interesting. She has a graduate student in psychology working at the camp this summer. She's writing a paper about the connection between riding horses and past violence. I told her that you were totally nonviolent, never even hit as a toddler. Isn't that fascinating? Oh, honey," she said, giving her daughter a hug. "I'm just so proud of you, I could burst."

"I've got to practice my piano." Wren slipped out of her mother's arms and took off running for her house.

"What on earth is the matter with her?" Aunt Leora asked.

"Probably just anxious to practice her piano. You know what a workaholic she is."

"Oh. Well, won't she be happy when I tell her that I gave Lady Gregson my permission for her to play in the camp talent show."

CHAPTER 11

Da, da, da, ping.

"Here," Wren said, hitting the right note on the piano. *Da, da, da, da.*

I tried again. *Da, da, da, ping.*

"Like this." Wren played the melody with her right hand. "See, it's easy."

"Easy for Mozart maybe," I mumbled.

Wren picked up my hand and placed it in the correct position on the piano. "And one and two and three go," Wren sang out in her high, sweet voice. "Come on. *Da, da, da, da. Da, da, da, da,*" she crooned.

I played. *Da, da, ping, da. Da, da, da, ping.*

"You're missing the syncopation."

"Sounds to me more like I'm missing the notes."

"Come on. You're getting it now."

Actually, what I was getting was older. But if Wren could write a paper on some ancient Greek war, the least I could do was learn to play one lousy tune on the piano. *Da, da, ping, ping.* Maybe.

Wren and I continued to work together until ten o'clock when Aunt Leora got home from her dinner date. Luckily, she kicked me out immediately, and I didn't have to think about the piano until the next day when Wren met me at the gate.

"Look," she said triumphantly. She was carrying a long, thin box under her arm. She flipped it open. "It's an electronic keyboard. You can use it at the store when you're not waiting on customers."

"Or if they're endlessly browsing and I want to drive them out."

Wren closed up the box. "I'll leave it in the tree house."

I handed her my softball glove. "Can you stick this in the tree house, too? Dad found it in Chuck's drawer while I was supposed to be playing softball, and I had to come up with a complicated story."

"You mean lie."

"Well, if you want to get technical about it."

Wren studied her hands. "I know. It's horrible," she burst out. "I've told more lies since we started this than I have in my entire life."

"I bet," I said. Unlike me, Wren was an unrepentant truth teller.

"So, what do you tell your father about your mornings?" Wren asked.

"You know, that I'm playing first base, making home runs." I cleared my throat. "Team star."

Wren shook her head and made little tsk sounds. "That's going to get you in trouble, too. Doesn't he want to see you play? He went to practically all of Pierce's school games."

"I told him that in the summer league, the games were closed to parents."

"And he believed that?"

I shrugged. "He hasn't shown up. Not that I'd know if he did show up since I'm not there. And there's no 'there' anyway, because as far as I know there's no girls' summer league."

"Don't you feel guilty?" Wren said, twirling her hair. "I do."

"I guess I do a little. Especially about lying to Dad. By the way, I told Ann your paper was brilliant."

"I don't know about brilliant, but I'm having a great time working on it," Wren said, brightening up. "I'm ending up writing about Thucydides. He wrote the *History of the Peloponnesian War*, you know."

I could feel my eyes glazing over. "Can't say that I did."

"Well, in the paper not only do I write about Thucydides, I tell the history of the war, which was really, really interesting," Wren said earnestly. "In 431, that's B.C., of course, the great city-states of Sparta and Athens—"

"Wren."

"What?"

"I don't care."

"You know what's wrong with you, Gracie? You don't know how to have fun."

"Just don't have so much fun that you make it too good, because even though I told Ann it was great, it has to sound like her."

"So it should read," Wren said, imitating Ann, "'the Peloponnesian War was like, a really, really big battle.'"

"Stop it," I said, giggling.

"Don't laugh. I've been helping Pierce with his English essay. And that's exactly what his stuff sounds like." She began to backtrack, "Well, not that bad. And, anyway, he's a terrific guy. . . ."

"I know you have a great brother," I soothed. "So, Pierce has a lot of academic stuff to make up this summer?"

"If he wants to be a senior this fall he has to pass his math final, come up with a biography for social studies, and write a personal essay for English."

"Ooh. Poor Pierce. Maybe he could just have your dad buy the school a chemistry lab or something."

"That's his plan for college."

"Really?"

"Nah. Some school will want him for their baseball or soccer team. But he has to graduate from high school first."

The black limousine pulled into the gates. Lance got out of the car and waved to Wren, while speaking into his cell phone. "I am trying to meet him. Yes, yes. I know the new moon is the deadline." He paused. "Okay. I will take care of it." He clicked off.

"Work," he said in an annoyed voice. "Hi, Gracie," he said to Wren, while pulling a lollipop out of his pocket. "I brought a lolly for your little brother."

"Thank you," Wren squealed, taking the lollipop. "That's so considerate."

"It's bad for his teeth," I said.

Lance ignored me. "I'd like to meet the little guy," he said to Wren.

"I don't even remember telling you about Chuck," Wren said, smiling prettily. "But if you want, I'll bring him to meet you later this week."

"Do you need a ride somewhere this morning?" he asked Wren.

"No, thank you."

"I need a ride to camp," I said, opening the back door and hopping into the limousine.

Lance reached over and swung the limousine door closed.

"Hey," I yelled. No one answered or even heard me. I opened the door.

"Really," Lance was saying. "I'm happy to take you as soon as I drop, uh, uh—"

"Wren," I said from inside the car.

"Off."

*   *   *

It drizzled all morning. As soon as I got home, I pulled Wren's keyboard down from the tree house, dried off the box, and put it under my bed. Grabbing a plum, I biked to the store, making it just before the heavy rains started. Dad and Chuck were there waiting for me.

Dad sniffed the air. "I smell horses."

Whoops. I usually swim and change out of my camp jeans before going to the store. But because of the rain, I forgot. "There were pony rides after softball." I jogged into the store bathroom to wash my hands, smooth out my tangled hair, and adjust my glasses.

"In the rain? Anyway, aren't fourteen-year-old girls a little old for pony rides?" Dad said when I came back out.

"It was just drizzling, and you're never too old for ponies," I said.

"How's the softball going?"

"Great." I pretended to pitch a ball. "Striking them out."

"I thought you played first base."

"I mean my team, the Polar Bears."

119

"Grizzlies," Dad said.

"Right, I always mix up my bears. Look at Chuck," I said, desperate to change the topic.

At the front of the store, Chuck was talking a woman into buying some lobster forks. "You can feed your dolls with them," he was telling her.

The lady handed him twenty dollars. "He's just adorable," she said, leaving.

Chuck ran over to me grinning broadly.

"Good going, Chuck," I said. "You are a natural." I held my hand up to give him a high five, but he gave me an enormous karate chop instead.

"Ow!" I cried. I made a grab for my little brother, but he scampered behind Dad.

"No hitting," Dad said to Chuck.

"I wasn't hitting. I was chopping. I am Prince Chopper and I will chop you up with my hands of steel," he said, waving his arms around.

"Your hands of steel will have a time out if they don't control themselves," Dad said. "Now apologize to your sister."

Chuck looked at his hands and made a sad face. "Sorry," he said to me.

"Okay," Dad said. "That was a good sale. Now

that Gracie's here, how about that ice-cream cone I promised you?"

"Yes, yes, yes, yes, yes!" Chuck yelled, dragging him out the door. It made a big creaking sound as it closed.

I was dusting a bookcase when Ann, Kip, and Vernon walked in. They were about as welcome as an outbreak of acne.

"Oh, hi, Wren," Ann said. "What are you doing here?"

Like she didn't know. "I work here."

"Why you work?" Kip asked.

"Same reason everyone else works. Money."

"Your parents don't give you money?" Vernon asked.

"There's a concept, huh?" I said. "So, how come you're not at camp?"

"It was raining, so the counselors organized a spontaneous field trip," Ann said.

"And all the museums were closed?" I said sourly.

"We thought about going to the Whaling Center, but Ann wanted to shop," Vernon said.

"Alone," Ann said. "I wanted to shop alone."

"I won't bother you," Vernon said.

"Err," Ann said, covering her face with her hands. Vernon had decided that he and Ann were meant for each other, and there was nothing Ann could say or do to discourage him. Not that she didn't try.

"You study piano in afternoon, no?" Kip said to me.

"Usually. But today piano was canceled because of the weather."

"Weather affects piano?" Kip said.

"My teacher has a pathological fear of water," I said. I crossed my arms and silently dared anyone to challenge me. No one did.

As long as they were here, I might as well make some sales. "Look around," I said in a friendlier voice. "There's lots of fun, funky stuff. And since you guys are friends, I'll give you a ten percent discount."

In short order, I talked Vernon into buying a bud vase for his mother's birthday and Ann into a pair of earrings made out of seashells. I was wrapping Vernon's gift while trying to sell Kip a set of toy soldiers when Chuck and Dad walked in carrying ice-cream cones. "Everybody," I said, thinking quickly, "I'd like you to meet some members of my family, Joe and Chuck Wright. And this is Ann, Kip, and Vernon."

"We know you," Chuck said to Ann.

"Ah yes. Wren's friend," my father said with a slight frown. He excused himself to work in the back.

Kip bent down to talk to Chuck. "The little boy, Charles Quicksilver Wright, yes?" he asked in an excited voice.

"I am not a little boy. I am Prince Chopper," Chuck said, "'cause of my hands of steel."

"Prince Chopper?" Kip looked puzzled.

"I'd show you how they work, but Dad's real mean about time-outs and, anyway, I'd drop my cone," Chuck said.

"I do not understand," Kip said.

Aunt Leora walked in, followed by Pierce. "My, you're having a busy day," Aunt Leora said.

"Hello," I squeaked.

"Hello, Mrs. Baldwin," Ann said. She turned to my cousin. "Hi, Pierce," she said, a big goofy grin covering her face. When she turned, she accidentally knocked her new earrings off the counter. She and Vernon bent down to pick them up and bumped heads.

"Don't help me," Ann said to Vernon angrily.

"I just talked to your mother," Aunt Leora said to Ann. "Who are your friends?"

Ann, who was rubbing her head and scowling at Vernon, didn't say anything.

"Ann. Your friends," Aunt Leora repeated.

"Oh, right," she said, coming out of it. "This is Kip Koravitch and Vernon Daniels." She gestured to them.

"You're Wren's mother?" Vernon asked.

Aunt Leora turned to Vernon. I held my breath, hoping I wouldn't get found out. "That's right. Daniels, Daniels," she mused. "Are you the son of Marietta Howell-Daniels?"

"Yes, ma'am," Vernon said.

"Your mother and I are on the town beautification committee together." She extended her hand to Vernon. "It's very nice to meet you, Vernon."

"So, Gracie," she said, turning to me, "where is your dad?"

I shrugged. "Don't know. But if you want Joe, he's in the back."

"This family," Aunt Leora said. Shaking her head in annoyance, she walked to the back of the store.

"You are Wren. Why she call you Gracie?" Kip asked.

"Silly family nickname," I said.

"What kind of nickname is Gracie?" Vernon inquired.

"Well," I said, improvising, "Monday's child is full of grace and I was born on a Monday, so that's my family nickname."

I glanced nervously over at Chuck, but he wasn't paying attention. He was holding his cone in his right hand and chopping imaginary enemies with his left. Pierce was all ears, though.

"Tuesday's child is full of grace. Monday's child is fair of face," Kip recited, giving me a sharp look.

"Well, uh, Gracie sounds better than Facie. How do you know that, anyway? I thought you were, like, Russian."

"In my country, we learn rhyme for English memorization."

"Actually, my cousin's name is Gracie," I said. "Gracie Wright."

"What is cousin like?" Kip asked.

"She's an awful girl," Ann said. "Isn't she, Wren?"

"Don't say bad things about my cousin Facie," Pierce said.

"You're so loyal," Ann cooed, smiling at Pierce.

"I'm very loyal, too," Vernon said to Ann.

"I don't understand," Kip said.

"You know, faithful, trustworthy, a true friend," Vernon explained to Kip.

"Gracie is just a nickname," I clarified.

"There must be much puzzlement at family dinners," Kip said.

"You wouldn't believe it," Ann said. "At the last family dinner, Wren's aunt announced that—"

"All right," I said loudly, cutting her off. "Let's not clutter up the store. I'm working here."

"Aha!" Chuck yelled. He leaped into the air and karate-chopped a book onto the floor. "Take that, you dustily villain."

"Dastardly," I corrected.

My mother walked into the store. Chuck bowed to her, accidentally bending his head into his chocolate cone. "Prince Chopper, Your Magnificence," he said, his face full of ice cream.

"Hello, sweetheart," Mom said, wiping his forehead. "I have just received a message from outer space."

I clapped my hands together noisily. "Come on. The store is way too crowded. Could everyone not buying anything please leave?" I called out.

"You mean like from aliens?" Vernon asked her in an excited voice.

"Of course," she said, like the answer was self-evident.

"Joe's in the back," I said weakly to my mother.

"Believing in aliens is silly," Kip said firmly.

"I believe in aliens," Vernon said. "Because they're definitely out there."

"I believe that aliens are in this store, right now," Ann said.

"I remember you," Mom said to Ann in an unfriendly voice.

"You guys have got to go," I said again.

"Some way to treat customers," Ann said to me.

"What do you think about Roswell and Area Fifty-one?" Vernon asked my mother.

My mother sniffed. "That stuff is just make-believe."

"What about crop circles, then?"

"Play with me, Mommy," Chuck said, pulling on her hand.

"I'll take him," Pierce said. He bent down, picked up my brother, and took a bite of his cone.

"Hey," Chuck said.

"Come on, Prince Chopper," Pierce said, walking out of the store with Chuck in his arms.

"I'll help you," Ann said, following Pierce like he was a giant magnet. "I love children." She tripped over her sneaker lace, banging into the counter.

"Wait for me, Ann," Vernon said, grabbing his package. "I love children, too."

Kip looked down at my mother. "Mrs. Quicksilver Wright, yes?"

Mom suddenly focused her eyes on the ceiling like she was receiving a message that no one else could hear. The pendant around her neck was flashing orange, two short flashes followed by a long one. "The time of danger is upon us," she said. Her eyes zeroed in on Kip. "Who did you say you were?"

"I go now," Kip said. He walked briskly out the door.

"He must love children, too," I said.

"You forgot to curtsy, Royal Miss," Mom said to me as the door squeaked closed. "What happened to the little girl who used to have the best curtsy this side of Polaris?"

I put my hands over my face. "You've got to stop, Mom. Please."

"It's important, especially at state occasions." Mom marched into the back of the store. "I need to discuss the situation with Dad right away. You and Charles are to be very careful."

I collapsed into the chair behind the counter. A few minutes later Pierce and Chuck walked back into the shop.

"Welcome to the cuckoo's nest," I said.

"Oh yeah," Pierce said, putting Chuck down. "That was quite a performance. I know what's going on, you know."

I put my forefinger up to my mouth and gestured to Chuck.

"Okay, later," he said, getting my message. "I

was telling Ann how I had to write a biography for social studies," he said, changing the subject. "She's been doing research on this guy named Thudiddies or something who wrote about, uh . . ."

"Thucydides and the Peloponnesian War," I said.

"That's right. How did you know that?"

"It's a popular subject," I said.

My mother floated through the store and toward the door, followed by Dad, Aunt Leora, and Chuck.

"Daddy is taking us home, and I'm going to make mud pies," Chuck said.

"The wormhole is open but very unstable," Mom said.

"Time to get started on your fall wardrobe," Aunt Leora said to Pierce.

"With grass on top for icing," Chuck said.

"Orange for danger. Red for destruction," Mom said.

"Maybe some chinos," Aunt Leora said, opening the squeaky screen door.

"Gotta oil that door," Dad said, exiting.

"Well, your mom may be odd, but at least she's

never boring," Pierce said after everyone left. "I wish my mother were more interesting."

"That's funny," I said to my cousin. "I wish mine were a little duller."

That night, after Chuck went to sleep, I set up my keyboard on the wooden picnic table behind our trailer and began practicing. About a half hour later my parents came outside to join me.

"If music be the food of love, you'd starve to death," Mom commented.

"Well, hopefully I'll improve."

"If it will make you feel better, I don't think you can get much worse," Mom said. She sat down next to me and smoothed my hair.

Dad plopped down on my other side. Suddenly I knew I was in trouble.

"So what's going on?" Dad asked.

Make that big trouble. "Nothing. I just need to know how to play the piano," I said.

"When?"

"Soon."

"Does this have anything to do with your mysterious mornings?" Dad asked.

My voice cracked. "What do you mean?"

"I mean that you disappear every morning," Dad said softly.

"I'm in the girls' softball league."

"Oh, Gracie," Dad said. "There is no girls' softball league. I know, I checked."

CHAPTER 12

It was about twenty minutes later and I had just finished explaining. First, I tried lying, but it was no use. They knew. Chuck saw Wren in the tree house while she was supposed to be at camp, and Dad found my muddy riding boots. The thing about pricking Ann just slipped out.

"So, Ann actually said, 'Who will be brave enough to ride the horse of a different color?'" Mom asked. She was sitting next to me at the picnic table. Dad had gotten up and was pacing back and forth in front of us.

"You are missing the point, Dotty," Dad said.

"No. You are missing the point," Mom said emphatically. A wisp of her tawny hair escaped from her bun and she brushed it back. She leaned forward and spoke earnestly. "The point is that the Maluxziads are getting ready to attack. I got another message from Nanny Goldstein."

"Nanny Goldstein?" Dad said.

"Earth name of Mom's secret agent," I said, earning a glare from Dad.

"Don't you start," Dad said to me.

"Just trying to explain," I said.

"Nanny Goldstein said that four Maluxziad fish creatures have landed on Earth," Mom continued. "Two are now disguised as humans. Their plan is to kidnap me, along with Gracie and Charles, bring us back to Pannadeau to renounce the throne, then kill us."

"Dotty," Dad said.

"Not that there's even a throne to renounce anymore. But the Maluxziads always hated loose ends." She sighed. "A strange and mysterious race."

"Can we get back to the matter at hand?" Dad said.

"When I made it through the wormhole, I

knew it hadn't closed forever. I even hoped to go back someday," Mom said, her eyes filling with tears. "And now, the wormhole is open. Beware of what you wish for."

"Enough," Dad said to Mom, rubbing his forehead. "I know you're upset, but we have a crisis here"—he shot a sharp look at Mom—"with earthlings on planet Earth."

"Would you sit down then, Gallant Consort? You're making me dizzy."

"Call me Joe, Dotty," Dad said.

"Joe. And Joe, I think two of the Maluxziads look like goats."

Dad squished his eyes closed, shook his head as if to clear it, and took a deep breath. "To get back to Earth"—Dad pulled out a chair and sat down—"this is how I see it. Although Wren was a full whatchamacallit in this plan, what it really means is that the Wrights stole money from the Baldwins."

"I didn't steal money from the Baldwins," I said.

"Were they planning on sending you to camp?" Dad asked.

I studied my fingernails. "No."

"A ritzy, expensive camp?"

"No."

"Run by a countess."

"Daughter of a duke and a princess."

"Are you sure you pricked Ann hard?" Mom asked.

"Dotty!" Dad snapped.

"Positive," I said.

"Clever of you to come up with the bee sting idea," Mom said.

Dad stood up and banged his fist on the table. "I said enough. And I meant it!"

Mom and I stared at Dad in shock. Occasionally Dad yelled at Chuck or me, but I don't think I ever heard him shout at Mom.

"Now," Dad said in a calmer voice, turning back to me. "What we have to do is to tell Wren's parents what is going on. Not about the Maluxziads," Dad said, holding up his hand, "about the camp. Then we apologize for our part in it and pay them back for the days Gracie was there."

He pointed his finger at me, jabbing it in the air for emphasis. "That means no allowance until every dime is paid back to the Baldwins. Do you understand?"

"Yes, Dad."

"Tomorrow you are to speak to Lady—what did you say her name was?"

"Gregson. Lady Gregson."

"Lady Gregson," Mom said thoughtfully. "I think she's Victoria—"

"Tomorrow, Gracie," Dad said, interrupting Mom, "you speak to Lady Gregson and tell her the truth. I'll meet you at the camp, so you won't have to do it alone."

"I'd like to go with you, too," Mom said. "I think I can help."

"Only on the condition that you keep the conversation limited to what's happening on this planet," Dad said.

Mom nodded. "All right."

"I mean it, Dotty. And we need to speak with Leora and Thomas," Dad said.

"Uncle Thomas is away on business," I said.

"I'll talk to Leora," Dad said.

"Before you explain, can I tell Wren what's going on?" I asked Dad.

"Okay. You tell Wren, then I'll go inside and talk to Leora." Dad took my hand and pulled me to my feet. "Come on. We'll do it now and get it over with."

We walked across the lawn to what Dad called the Mansion and Mom called the Big Ugly. Dad walked slowly with his head down and his hands in his pockets. "Stabbing another girl. I thought you had more sense than that."

"I do. I mean, I'm sorry."

Dad shook his head. "What were you thinking?"

"I don't know. It's stupid. Mom's been making me practice every night. Then, when Ann said the thing about the horse of a different color I just pulled out my Maluxziad pricker and let her rip."

"Oh, Gracie," Dad said softly. "That is so not okay. And the fact that you and Mom have been practicing, makes it so much more . . . whatcha-macallit . . . purposeful, I guess.

"I love your mother so very much," Dad said. "I wish I could afford to buy her a palace and jewels fit for the queen she is inside. But"—squaring his shoulders, Dad continued—"but you and Chuck are my life. And I simply can't have you sticking an innocent girl with a what-did-you-call-it, a

Maluxziad pricker, because you're caught up in Mom's crazy world." His voice broke. "I can't."

"I'm sorry, Daddy. I am. I just got carried away. You know I don't believe it. But Ann said that thing . . . and . . ." My voice trailed off.

"And Chuck is playing all these make-believe games where he's King This and Prince That." Dad paused. "The other day he was stabbing enemy water balloons with a hat pin."

I gasped. Mom must have given Chuck his own pricker. "She promised. . . ."

"What?" he said sharply.

I shook my head. "Nothing."

"Your aunt Leora thinks your mother is headed for a nervous breakdown and that I should take her back to Barking Tree."

"Are you going to?"

Dad shook his head but didn't answer. We walked up the white stone path. The Baldwins' house was all lit up, and there was a fancy car in the driveway. "Looks like Leora has company," Dad said.

I looked over at Dad. He was wearing his work clothes, old jeans and a torn T-shirt, which were stained with turpentine and paint. He hadn't shaved in several days and his work boots were filthy. "You probably shouldn't go in yet," I said.

"Why? Because then my sister wouldn't get to serve on her garden-library-museum benefit committee gala-thingy if her high-class buddies got wind of her brother?"

"That's not like you, Dad."

He shook his head and sighed. "I know."

"We should talk to Wren first, anyway," I said. With a practiced hand, I threw a pebble at Wren's window. A couple of seconds later, the window flew open and Wren looked out.

"Throw down the rope ladder," I said in a loud whisper. "We need to talk."

"Okay," Wren said. She hooked the ladder to her window and threw it down.

Dad gave it an experimental tug to make sure it was fastened securely, then sat down in the grass under Wren's window. "You go. Talk to Wren. I'm going to sit here and think for a few minutes."

"Okay." I patted him on the shoulder. "Throw a pebble up when you want me."

I began to climb up the rope ladder. But before

I could get to the window, the front door opened with a bang. A second later the outdoor floodlights snapped on, lighting up the house and gardens. I froze in place hanging on the side of the house.

"How dare you?" Leora screamed, following a tall dark-haired woman to the driveway. "Get off my property." She pointed at the woman's car. "Go!"

Heels crunching on the gravel, the woman walked swiftly toward her car. When she passed Dad she let out a high-pitched shriek.

Dad waved. "Nice night."

"What are you doing here?" Aunt Leora yelled at Dad.

The woman shrieked again, pointing to the side of the house. I was hanging just underneath Wren's window, clutching the rope ladder.

I waved. "Hi, Aunt Leora," I said.

Wren waved, too. "Hi, Mom."

"You stabbed my child," the woman yelled at Wren.

The light dawned. "Mrs. Armstrong?" I asked.

The lady glared up at me. "Who wants to know?"

"Wren told me the story. She didn't stab anyone. She was just swatting at a bee, and the bee stung your daughter."

"See," Aunt Leora said triumphantly. "I told you my baby wouldn't hurt a fly."

"This place is a nuthouse," Mrs. Armstrong said, getting into her car.

"She should come to my house," I said to Wren.

Rolling down her window, Mrs. Armstrong yelled, "Ann told me that she was stabbed and my daughter doesn't lie." With that, she sped down the driveway.

"Leora. I need to talk to you," Dad said.

"That was Elizabeth Armstrong. Granddaughter of a Roosevelt." Aunt Leora's voice shook. "She said I was a lousy mother. And," her voice dropped to a whisper, "a social-climbing sycophant."

"What's a social-climbing sycophant?" I asked Wren under my breath.

"It's like the grown-up version of sucking up to the popular girls," Wren whispered back.

Aunt Leora stood in the driveway with her hands over her eyes. Dad went over to her and put his arms around her. "It's all right," he said, patting her back gently.

For a moment Aunt Leora hung there. She looked up at Dad and wiped her eyes. "You're a good brother, Joe," she said, her voice breaking. Moving quickly, she walked to her car. "Gracie, Joe, go home. I've got to see Dr. Bosco."

"Dr. Bosco?" I said.

"Mom's guru. He's got spiky hair and smells like a muskrat," Wren said.

"Deep healing breaths," Aunt Leora said. She expelled air noisily.

"I need to talk to Wren," I called from my ladder.

"And I need to talk with you about Wren's camp," Dad said to Aunt Leora.

"You need. You need." Aunt Leora spun around, pointing first at me, then at Dad. "Well, I need to pull myself together first. Can't you see that?" She flung her arms to the heavens. "Can't you all just see that?" She walked over to her car. "Social-climbing sycophant," she muttered to herself as she climbed in and slammed the car door shut.

"You'd better come down," Dad said to me as

Aunt Leora drove off. He looked up at Wren in the window. "Are you going to be all right here, Niece, or would you like to stay over with us?"

"I'm fine. Pierce and Blanca are here. Anyway, I'm fourteen."

"Okay." Dad nodded. "Listen, Wren, you and Gracie have been found out."

"Found out?" Wren turned white.

"Your aunt Dorothea and I know that you and Gracie switched places and that she's been going to camp instead of you."

"You can't tell Mom. She'll go nuts."

"Go nuts," I said.

"Like your mother's normal."

"Watch it," I said.

"I'll help you with your mom," Dad said gently. "But it must be done. Come on, Gracie," he continued, waving me down. "Time to go home. Get a good night's sleep."

I scrambled down the rope ladder. "For tomorrow is going to be a horrible day," I said.

CHaPTeR 13

The next morning Wren met me at the gate as we had planned. Chuck, who was acting cranky, came along with me. He sat on the ground and wrapped himself around my leg like sticky tape on a mailer.

I was feeling pretty cranky myself. The plan was that I was to go to camp as usual. Dad didn't want to send me, but I managed to talk him into it. My arguments were that I didn't know how to cancel the limousine and that Wren couldn't show up before we talked to Lady Gregson, anyway.

"No riding. No camp activities," Dad instructed. "I plan on speaking to Leora as soon as she gets home. But whether I reach her or not, your days as a camper are over."

I begged to be allowed to have one last ride, but Dad stood firm. I knew I had done the wrong thing, and, like Dad said, I had to take responsibility for my actions. Still, one last ride wouldn't hurt anybody.

As I waited for the limo, I tried to tell Wren about my conversation with my father, but it was clear that she was barely paying attention. She paced back and forth in front of the gate alternately twirling and chewing on a lock of hair. "This is going to be so awful" was about all she could say.

I made an effort to comfort her. "Maybe your mother will find the situation amusing."

"Maybe an orange dog will fall out of the sky and eat me," Wren said.

"Maybe there really are aliens," I said.

The long black limousine pulled through the gates. "Look on the bright side. Starting tomorrow, you'll get to ride to camp with your boyfriend." I made little kissing noises.

Wren scowled at me. "Lance is not my boyfriend. And, did anyone ever tell you that you have the maturity level of a hatchling?"

"Can't say they have," I said. I leaned down to pry Chuck off my leg. "I've got to go. Can you take Cling the Child home?" I pulled Chuck up and passed him over to Wren.

"Don't call me Cling," Chuck whined. "I'm King Punch Your Guts Out, the Fierce."

"Stop it," I said to Chuck. "You're not king anything. You're Charles Wright, a regular boy."

"Not," Chuck pouted.

"Are," I snapped.

Chuck wrapped his legs around Wren's waist, draped his arms over her shoulders, dropped his head, and closed his eyes. "Not," he whined into her shoulder.

Lance got out of the limousine. "Good morning," he said to Wren. "Is that your little brother?"

"That's Chuck Wright," I replied.

"Lift your head up so I can see you, little fellow," Lance said.

Chuck looked up at Lance for a moment, then flopped back down.

"He's tired. He was out on a late date last night," I said to Lance.

Lance didn't even crack a smile. Instead, he

tapped his watch and walked back to his limousine. "Can I drop you somewhere this morning?" he asked Wren.

"No, thank you," Wren said, dropping her eyes.

"But starting tomorrow, my darling, you can drop me off every day," I whispered softly, aiming my words directly into Wren's ear.

She gave me a little shove. If looks could kill, I'd be one dead hatchling.

Wren told Lance that because we were cousins, we were taking turns going to camp. Starting Monday it was her turn.

Lance accepted her explanation without a question. So handsome, yet so stupid.

The ride to camp was unusual because Lance spoke on his cell phone the entire time. The window between us was up so I couldn't hear anything, but I could tell that he was excited.

As soon as Lance dropped me off at camp, I ran down to the stable to talk to Flash.

The black gelding whinnied happily when he saw me. I hugged him, breathing in the robust perfume of horse. "Pretend you are Lady Gregson," I told Flash. He nosed my pocket, where I had several carrots and sugar cubes hiding.

"Why, Lady Gregson, get your nose out of my pocket," I said, giggling. "And no drooling, please." I fed Flash a carrot. "Now pay attention, horse. I'm not the incredibly wealthy Wren Baldwin. Yes," I said, pretending to answer his question, "I do mean the department store Baldwins. My real name is Gracie Wright. I'm here under false pretenses, and I'm as poor as dirt."

Except for the occasional nicker, my explanation of how my cousin and I switched places went down quite well with Flash. I just hoped Lady Gregson would be as accepting. Thinking about telling her the story made my stomach churn.

A few minutes later her sharp morning call cut the air. "Wish me luck, now, horse." Flash neighed softly and rubbed his head against my shoulder. My eyes welled up as I gave him a hug. "Good-bye, Flash." Walking slowly, I dragged myself up the hill toward the flagpole.

Officer Sharpe showed up at the morning meeting. She stood behind Lady Gregson, her eyes darting from camper to camper as if at any moment she expected one of us to get up and commit a felony. At one point Officer Sharpe looked at me, raised her eyebrows, and tapped her nose in a meaningful manner.

Kids were leaving to go to their activities when she grabbed me by the arm. "Come with me, young lady," Officer Sharpe said in my ear as she marched me toward Lady Gregson's office.

"Hey, look. Wren's in trouble," Vernon said.

"What did you do? Rob a bank?" Ann yelled.

"Down with the police-state camp!" Kip cried, waving his fist in the air.

Lady Gregson followed us into her office. "What's going on?" she asked Officer Sharpe. "I know you've been investigating some strange occurrences, but I don't think Wren Baldwin set off fireworks in the preserve, killed my goats, or sprayed graffiti on the roof. And I wish you could have asked her to come in here in a more subtle manner."

"This girl," Officer Sharpe said, shaking my arm, "is not Wren Baldwin. I found out yesterday, when I called Mrs. Armstrong about the stabbing."

"It was a bee!" I yelled.

"You called a camper's mother and told her that her daughter had been stabbed?" Lady Gregson said in an outraged voice.

"That's right." Officer Sharpe stood her ground.

"There is no evidence that this girl stabbed anyone, as stabbing implies a wound and a weapon, and frankly," Lady Gregson said, "I saw neither. Furthermore, you have overstepped your boundaries and I—"

"In the course of conversation," Officer Sharpe interrupted, "Mrs. Armstrong said something about Wren's long blonde hair. Concerned about the discrepancy, I called the headmaster at Whitmore Prep—that's her school—and got this picture."

Officer Sharpe reached into her jacket pocket and pulled out a picture of my cousin. She threw it on Lady Gregson's desk. "This is the real Wren Baldwin." She looked at me triumphantly. "The nose is never wrong."

Lady Gregson walked over to her desk and examined the picture. "I've suspected you weren't

Wren Baldwin for some time," Lady Gregson said to me, sitting down. She folded her dirt-stained hands under her chin.

"You have?" I said softly.

"Your mother described an overly cautious, antisocial, rather dreamy girl, and if I may say so, you are nothing like her description."

I hung my head.

"So," Lady Gregson said, "just who are you?"

Officer Sharpe slapped her nightstick into her open palm. "She's a common thief." She paused as the stick cracked into her hand. "And a liar."

I stared down at the floor. "I'm Gracie Wright."

"Wright," Lady Gregson said thoughtfully. "I know that name."

At first slowly, then picking up speed as I explained, I told Lady Gregson the whole story.

"So. All this time you've been pretending to be your cousin?" Lady Gregson asked.

"Yes, ma'am."

Officer Sharpe cracked her nightstick again. "Guilty."

"Good morning, Lady Gregson." All eyes turned to the door as my mother swept in. Following behind her were Dad, Chuck, and Wren. "I'm sure your father, the great duke of Landtonvelt, would counsel mercy."

Lady Gregson stared at my mother. "Queenie."

"Lady Bug," my mother replied. Then they did the most amazing thing. They curtsied, gave each other high fives, bumped their behinds, and embraced.

Lady Gregson shook hands warmly with my father. "Joe."

"Victoria," Dad said. "You're Lady Gregson?"

"You believe this?" I whispered to Wren.

Wren, whose mouth was hanging open, shrugged.

"Gracie Wright, you are under arrest for theft of services," Officer Sharpe said.

"Forget it," Lady Gregson said.

"What?" Officer Sharpe yelped. "The girl is a thief."

"I propose to make her stay a scholarship," Lady Gregson said.

"I knew there was something wrong with her the first moment I saw her," Officer Sharpe said.

"A scholarship! Wow," I said.

"Prosecute!" yelled Officer Sharpe, practically jumping up and down.

"That's very generous, my lady," Mom said.

"No," Dad said. He spoke with such command that everyone in the room turned to look at him. "That is not okay with me. Gracie did a bad thing, and if she's to learn something there must be a whatchamacallit."

"Consequence," Wren said.

Thank you, dictionary woman, I thought.

"Jail time," Officer Sharpe said, rubbing her hands together.

"How about a chain gang?" I said sarcastically.

"Quiet, Gracie," Dad said.

"What do you suggest, Joe?" Lady Gregson asked.

"Maybe a few days mucking out stalls?" Dad said.

"Really?" I said. "Can I?"

Wren elbowed me.

"Er, I mean gross," I said.

"Hmm," Lady Gregson said. "I don't want her here during the week while camp is in session. It would just be too confusing for the other campers, especially if Wren is here, too. But on the weekends the property is open for day guests. Although campers and their families sometimes come, most of the day guests are tourists."

"Saturdays are our busiest day at the store," Dad said, "and my wife doesn't drive. But Sundays we open late and close early, so I could take her then."

"Fine," Lady Gregson agreed. "How about Gracie works the next couple of Sundays?"

"That's good," Dad said.

"What about me?" Wren asked.

"Well, that's up to your parents and, of course, Lady Gregson," Dad said. "Though for you, I bet coming to camp will be punishment enough."

"I beg your pardon," Lady Gregson said to Dad.

"I apologize, Victoria," my father said to Lady Gregson. "I know from my daughter that you run a fine program."

"Gracie," Lady Gregson said, "why don't you show your cousin around the grounds while I work out the details with your parents."

"Okay." I grabbed Wren's hand and pulled her toward the door.

"I want to go, too," Chuck begged.

"Can I show him the horses, Lady Gregson?" I asked.

"Of course," she said.

"I'll go and keep an eye on them, shall I, Lady Gregson?" Officer Sharpe said.

"That won't be necessary. You may leave now," Lady Gregson said.

"Come on," I said to Wren. I took Chuck by the hand and raced out of the office. I was never so happy to get out of a room in all my life.

"All right," I said, doing a little jig in front of the administration building. "That went pretty well. And can you believe they know each other?"

Wren, who was slapping her arms nervously, didn't say anything.

The door of Lady Gregson's office opened and we heard the voice of Officer Sharpe. "You haven't seen the last of me. There's something odd going on at this camp. Gracie Wright is in the center of it, and by nose, I'm going to find out what it is." The door closed loudly, and a red-faced Officer Sharpe stepped into her patrol car and sped off.

"So, how come your mom didn't show up?" I

asked Wren as we headed over to the wooded trail that led to the stables.

"She called Blanca early this morning to say that she needed to stay at the retreat and work on her spit," Wren said.

"She's learning how to spit? Cool," Chuck said.

"She probably said spirit, and Blanca got it wrong." Wren gave a little snort of laughter. "Still, with my mom you never know."

We walked through the trail. "So, that means that Aunt Leora doesn't know what's going on yet, right?"

"Right." Wren began twirling her hair like a maniac.

I patted her back sympathetically. "I know. It's going to be hard."

Wren sighed. "No. It's going to be impossible. Plus it means I'm going to have to come here."

"It's a great place. You're going to love it, you'll see." We came out of the trail at the top of the hill. Separating us from the stables was a carpet of rippling meadow grass. "Horses!" Chuck yelled. He let go of my hand and began running down the hill. Luckily, I managed to grab the collar of his

T-shirt. With Chuck pulling me like a dog on a leash, we made it down to the stables.

Stedman, who was giving a lesson in the out-door ring, gave me a friendly wave.

"Boy, these horses are big," Wren said nervously.

"Don't worry. You're going to get Stout," I said. "He's more like an armchair than a horse. Come and meet him." Keeping a firm grip on Chuck, who was wriggling with excitement, I grabbed Wren with my other hand and dragged her over to Stout's stall. "Hi, Stout," I said. As usual Stout was standing statue still. "You want to give him a pat?" I asked Wren.

Wren's eyes widened as she looked up at the big bay. "Uh-uh," she said, shaking her head.

Chuck was jumping up and down. "I want to pat him."

"Let's give him a treat," I said. I took a sugar cube out of my pocket and gave it to my brother. "Here, Chuck. Just put your palm out flat and old Stout here will eat the sugar right off your hand."

Stout put his head down and ate the sugar cube.

"Ooh. It tickles. Did you see that? I fed a horse," Chuck said, grinning with delight.

"Here," I said to my brother, handing him some carrots. "Give him one at a time."

"Thanks." Chuck's face beamed as he continued feeding Stout.

"He's really big," Wren said again.

"Don't worry. Stout is gentle, and Stedman, who runs the stables, is really nice and patient."

"But not as fabulous as his grandson," Hart said, coming up behind us with Cinnamon on the lead and Dog behind them.

"Hi, Hart." I turned back to Wren. "This is Hart Stedman. He thinks he's fabulous, but mostly he's touchy."

"Touchy! Touchy? The nerve," Hart said with a grin.

Cinnamon walked over to Wren and put her head down. Her ears, which were usually back, perked up and she gave a friendly whinny.

"Wow," Hart said. "I've never seen Cinnamon do that before. She must like you."

"Great," Wren said, backing away.

"She wants to be patted," I said to Wren. "Remember, I told you about the abused horse Stedman and Hart were trying to heal. That's her. Cinnamon."

"Oh, poor horse," Wren said softly. Cinnamon whinnied at Wren again. Tentatively, Wren reached out and patted her neck and Cinnamon looked her in the eyes. Her head bobbed up and down like she was nodding. "Amazing," Wren said. "It's like Cinnamon is talking to me."

"She is," Hart said. "Maybe this shy, nervous girl is ready to come out of her shell a little."

"I don't think so," Wren said.

"He didn't mean you," I said, nudging Wren, who turned bright red.

Hart took a piece of apple out of his pocket and handed it to Wren. "Here, try feeding her."

Uncertainly, Wren took the fruit out of Hart's hand and fed it to Cinnamon.

"I want to feed her, too," Chuck said. He reached out to Cinnamon and she reared back.

"She's not ready for you yet," Hart said.

"This is my brother, Chuck," I said to Hart. "And I'll bet that few horses are ready for him."

"Well, Stout is," Hart said. He lifted Chuck up and put him on Stout's back. "How do you like that?" he asked my brother.

"I'm on a horse, I'm on a horse," Chuck sang.

"Here." Hart handed Stout's reins to me. "Let's walk him around. And you," he said, turning to Wren, "can lead Cinnamon."

"I don't know," Wren said.

"It's okay. If you need help, I'll be right next to you," Hart said.

Hesitantly, Wren took Cinnamon's reins. We began walking through the stable to the field outside.

"Hart, this is my cousin Wren."

"Wren and Wren," Hart said. "Must be a lot of confusion at family dinners."

"Actually, I'm Gracie." I kicked at the dirt with the toe of my boot. "You see," I began, then stopped and sighed. "Forget it," I muttered.

"It's okay," Hart said softly. "I know the story." He paused for a moment. "Uh, Flash told me."

I blushed. "You know it's not nice to eavesdrop on a person's conversation with a horse."

"Yeah. Well, I'd put it in my etiquette rule

book, if I weren't so touchy about it," he said, grinning. "So, uh, you aren't rich?"

I looked down at my boots. "Afraid not." I put my hand on Wren's arm. "My cousin here is the rich one."

"The one adjective about me everyone agrees on," Wren said wryly.

"There's also beautiful, nice, and smart," I said to her.

"So, does this mean you're not coming back to camp?" Hart asked me.

"No. You're still stuck with me," I said cheerfully. "In fact, I'm going to be a stable slave. For the next couple of Sundays, anyway."

Hart's face broke into a smile. "Just what we need. A girl who doesn't know how to do anything. Getting in the way, asking endless questions."

"Think of how I feel," I said, grinning back. "Working with Stedman's persnickety staff."

"So, now I'm persnickety?"

"See, touchy," I said to Wren. Then I grinned. "And, a little bit fabulous."

* * *

When we got home, I asked Mom how she knew Lady Gregson.

"I will tell you, but first I must swear you to secrecy."

"I promise."

"Blood oath." Mom gave me a stern look.

"I swear on the blood of my ancestors of the Realm of Pannadeau that I will reveal this secret to no one," I said, holding my palm up.

"I knew her at Barking Tree," Mom said. "In fact, we were roommates." She paused, remembering. "The staff called us the royals."

"So, Lady Gregson doesn't want anyone to know that she was in a mental institution?" I asked.

"If it weren't for her business, I don't think she'd care. Royalty doesn't mind being considered eccentric, you know. It's part of their charm."

"You saying something personal here?" I teased.

"Just because I don't hold the same beliefs as everyone else, does not make me eccentric. In this particular case, it makes everyone else wrong."

"Uh-huh."

"But people are entrusting their children to her and might not if they thought she was emotionally unstable. Not that she is. She was at Barking Tree for . . ." My mother stopped. "Personal family reasons."

"So no one was crazy there, right?"

"Some were, but not either of us." Mom smiled. "Once, she helped me break a toilet."

"What?" I said, confused.

"Long story. We're going to have tea and catch up as soon as the camp session ends."

"Really? Aunt Leora will die of jealousy."

"Speaking of that, Lady Gregson told me that most of the people who send their children or come on the weekends do so partially to meet her. They want to rub elbows with the queen's cousin. And although she's very gracious during business hours, she accepts no invitations except from other royals."

"Like you?"

"They don't call me the Magnificent Presence for nothing."

CHAPTER 14

On Sunday I was up and dressed at dawn. I dressed as noisily as possible—closing my drawers with a bang, rattling the medicine cabinet door—but no one else so much as stirred. I had to wait for almost two hours before Dad was up and ready to drive me to Camp Greenlong for my punishment.

Camp Greenlong was different on weekends, mostly because there was no camp. Instead, the grounds were open for paying guests. Visitors could ride, rent a sailboat, fish, play tennis, hike, or just lie out on the lawn and picnic.

Dad dropped me off by the administration office. On the way to the stables I passed Lady Gregson.

She was holding court by the flagpole, where she was cutting flowers from some hydrangea bushes. Her huge body was encased in a long bottle-green dress accessorized with scuffed hiking boots and a large flowered hat, and she was bellowing in her British accent. "How my old father, the duke, loved meat pies and red wine. Gave him a gouty toe, very painful you know. Ended his days a vegetarian in bedroom slippers, poor dear."

The guests hung on her every word. When Lady Gregson saw me, she walked over. Adjusting her hat so that no one but me could see her face, she spoke. "I trust that I can count on your discretion."

I nodded. "I'm very good at secrets."

"I believe that," Lady Gregson said dryly.

"Can I ask you something? What was my mother like when you knew her at Barking Tree?"

"Queenie?" Lady Gregson squeezed her lips together as she thought. "Well, she was a lovely person. Kind, beautiful, funny. And except for her claim that she was an extraterrestrial queen, quite normal."

"She said that she was at Barking Tree looking for something," I said.

"That's right. Some kind of necklace or amulet, I think. She put on quite a crazy act until she found it. Also, there was no way she was leaving Barking Tree without your dad." She smiled remembering. "Your mother fell in love with him the day he came to repair the doorknob to our room. It took him a while to fix it and when he was done, she was in love. Your dad, too, I think, but he was far too shy to say anything. So, your mother started breaking things—the idea being that your dad would be called in to fix them." Lady Gregson started to laugh. "I remember once I helped her damage a loo. We didn't know anything about plumbing, so we didn't break it intelligently, and it began to run like mad. By the time your father got there, we had flooded the basement."

"Really?"

"Really. He had to pump it out, then repair the damage. It took a week, and by the time it was fixed, they were engaged." She sighed. "It was very sweet."

Glancing at her watch, Lady Gregson told me that I'd better get down to the stables.

As soon as I arrived, Stedman put me to work, saddling up a group of horses for the morning trail ride. I didn't think that I was going to see any of the kids I knew from camp, but Vernon showed up as a day guest. "Hey, Wren," he said cheerfully. "Are you taking the trail ride, too?"

"No, I'm the help. One of the weekend stable boys had to go away for a family emergency," I lied, "so Lady Gregson hired me to work the next couple of Sundays."

"I forgot your parents didn't give you any money," Vernon said. "Though working in the stable sounds like fun. Maybe Lady Gregson could hire me, too."

"Great," Hart said, coming around the barn followed by Dog. "You can give me a hand mucking out the stalls."

"I don't mean today," Vernon said quickly. "Besides, I'm on the morning ride. I'm trying to get good enough to pass my trail test so I can ride the trails alone. Maybe take Ann."

Stedman walked out of the stables leading Spot. "Good morning, Vernon. I've got Spot saddled up and ready for you," he said.

As soon as Vernon walked away from us, Hart

leaned down and whispered in my ear, "Like he'd last five minutes."

Stedman put me on pony ride duty. My job was to lead Napoleon, an ancient, sweet animal, around the ring. That part was easy. The hard part was making sure that the little buckaroos, some nervous, some wildly enthusiastic, and some just wild, stayed in the saddle where they belonged.

"Guess what?" Vernon said, grinning when the trail ride came back. "I saw Kip hiking in the woods. Would you walk Spot so I can go back and find him?" Without waiting for me to agree, he handed me the reins and ran for the woods.

"You've got to cool Spot down," Hart called after him.

"Wren's doing it," he yelled.

"People like him really get me mad," Hart said. "Just because he's a rich day guest, he thinks you have to walk out his horse like a personal servant."

"You shouldn't judge people by their money. You know my cousin, the real Wren? Well, she's rich, but she's the nicest, smartest person I know."

"Yeah. Well I have to put up with people like

your friend Ann, who calls me stable boy and says snotty things to me."

"I told you she's not my friend and that's not right either. What I'm trying to say is that money is not a good yardstick for measuring people. Look at me. I'm the same person now when you know that I'm poor, as I was when you thought I was rich."

"And as obnoxious as ever, I might add," he said, winking.

By three o'clock I was pooped. I was leaning on Napoleon when Hart came over to me. "Tired? Want to take a little rest?"

I stood up straight. I could last more than five minutes, that was for sure. "No, I'm good. Full of energy," I lied.

"Fab," he said, clapping me on the shoulder. "I'll let Jimmy and Pete"—they were the other stable boys—"go home early then. You and I can feed the horses."

Me and my big mouth. "Great," I said, trying to look perky.

Stedman went into the barn office to work on the books, and Hart and I scooped grain and carried buckets of water into each stall. The pails were so heavy I thought my arms were going to fall off.

We had just finished when Lady Gregson came down to the stables. "Have you kids seen Vernon?" she asked.

"Last time I saw him, he was running into the woods to meet Kip," Hart said.

"Hmm. I didn't see Kip come in. Well, anyway, Vernon didn't come home when expected and his mom is worried," Lady Gregson replied. "I'll ask Stedman to search."

"Gramps went to pick up some vitamin pellets for Shimmer. Vernon and Kip like to hang out in the field past the woods. I'll go and round them up," Hart said, putting down his food scoop.

"Thank you. Take the cell and call me in my office when you find him," Lady Gregson said, handing a tiny black cell phone to Hart before starting back up the hill.

"Why did you lie about Stedman?" I asked when Lady Gregson was out of earshot.

Hart walked over to the barn office and put his finger over his lips. He cracked the door open. Stedman was sitting at his desk fast asleep. Carefully, so that the door wouldn't make a sound, he closed it. "He's getting older. His doctor says he should rest more, take it easy, so I try to see that he does. I'm all he has in the world and I need to look out for him." Hart walked out of the stables toward the woods on the other side of the pasture followed by Dog.

"I'll come, too," I called, trotting to catch up.

"No horse?" Hart said when I reached him.

"I'm not supposed to ride anymore."

"You can ride with me. That won't count." Hart gave me a leg up onto Dog's back, then leaped up in front of me.

"Put your arms around my waist so you don't fall," Hart said.

Tentatively, I put my hands on either side of his waist. I was glad I was behind him because I could feel myself blushing furiously.

The woods on this side of camp were thicker and darker, but the trail was well marked and Dog moved through it without hesitating. After about five minutes, the trees started to thin, then gave way to a huge pasture of high grass.

"Look," I said, pointing. Walking in what looked like a cut circle of grass was Vernon.

"Yo, Vernon," I yelled.

Vernon waved. "Come here," he called.

"Can you believe this," he said when Hart and I got to him. "Look at this grass. It's a perfect circle. I know. I measured."

"Your mother is worried about you," Hart said.

"I think I discovered a crop circle. An actual crop circle. Notice that the grass is flattened, not cut," Vernon said.

"I've got to call Lady Gregson," Hart said, digging the phone out of his pocket and dialing.

"Where's Kip?" I asked Vernon.

"I don't know. I saw the crop circle and stopped looking for him," Vernon said.

Hart spoke to Lady Gregson. While he was talking, I jumped off Dog and squatted down beside Vernon. The tall grass was indeed crushed. "Weird," I said, running my fingers over the compacted grass.

"Probably some kids playing around with a tractor," Hart said. He snapped the phone shut and put it back in his pocket. "We have to go."

"But there is no trail leading to it or away from it," Vernon said. "Tomorrow I'm going to bring my camera, get a picture, and send it to the Paranormal

Institute." He smiled dreamily. "I'll call it Vernon's Circle. Maybe be famous for finding it."

"Ha," Hart snorted.

"Ann will be so impressed."

"Hey. You know, a lot of reputable people believe in aliens," I said to Hart.

"You one of them?" Hart asked me.

"Not exactly," I said. "But I, uh . . ." Out of the corner of my eye, I saw a tall blond figure running. I spun around. "Someone is over there," I said.

Hart peered across the field. "Are you sure? I don't see anyone," he said.

"Maybe it's an alien!" Vernon said. As the three of us walked back to the stable followed by Dog, Vernon chattered a mile a minute about how the federal government used its power to cover up alien encounters. He sure knew a lot about it.

I was packing up to go when my father and brother showed up at the stable. "Dad. Chuck," I yelled, waving them over. Chuck threw his arms around my legs, knocking me off balance. I pulled him up for a hug. "I had a fantastic day," I said.

"So it was a good punishment and you learned your lesson?" Dad said.

"Oh. Right. It was a horrible day and I worked like an ox. But I didn't learn my lesson yet, so I'll have to come back next weekend."

"She did work hard, Mr. Wright," Hart said, coming up behind him. "And we really needed the extra help."

"And you are?"

"Hart Stedman. Tom Stedman's grandson. I work here."

Dad looked Hart up and down, then held out his hand. "Nice to meet you," he said, shaking hands. "Say hi, Chuck."

"Don't call me Chuck. I'm Judo Killer Man, king of the Judoarians."

"I met you before, King Judo Killer Man," Hart said, squatting down in front of him. Behind him, Dog whinnied. "I know you met Stout. But did you meet my horse, Dog?"

"That's funny," Chuck said, giggling. "Is your dog named Horse?" Then he began talking to himself. "And this is my arm, leg. And this is my finger, toe."

"How did the store do?" I asked Dad.

"Not as well as if you were there, but not bad," Dad said.

"We have an antique shop," I explained to Hart.

"This is my elbow, knee. And this is my front side, backside," Chuck continued, exploding with laughter.

I rolled my eyes. "He's five," I said to Hart.

"We've got to get going," Dad said.

"I want to pet Stout," Chuck said. "He's my favorite 'cause he ate my hand."

"Ate out of your hand," I corrected.

"And I rode him, too. Take me to him," he said, raising his arm grandly. "I command you."

I stood there with my arms folded. "Magic word."

"Please, please, please, please, please, please." He grabbed my hand and pulled me toward the stable.

I looked at my dad, who nodded okay.

"Mom says that if a person tries to snatch me, I should kick him as hard as I can, right in the shins," Chuck said, turning to Hart, who was following behind us as we walked. "If I were tall, like you," Chuck continued, "I could just strangle him."

"Mom shouldn't tell you stuff like that," I said to Chuck.

"If it's a Maluxziad, I'd just prick it, of course," Chuck said casually like he fought aliens every day. He tugged on Hart's arm.

"I'm the next king, you know."

"I thought you were already king," Hart said. "King of the Judomen or something."

"I mean in real life," Chuck said.

"That's nice," Hart said, humoring him.

"There's Stout," I said when we got to his stall. Hart lifted Chuck up so that he could feed the old bay a piece of carrot. Chuck didn't want to leave Stout, so finally Hart put him on Dog and together we led him back to where Dad was waiting.

"Too bad you're not going to be here tomorrow," Hart said as we walked.

"You mean it?" I asked.

"Yeah. Flash is going to miss you. Dog, too."

"Really?"

"Yeah." He paused. "Well, they'll look forward to seeing you next Sunday," Hart said.

"And I'll look forward to seeing them," I said. "And you, too," I whispered, but not loud enough for Hart to hear.

CHAPTER 15

The sun was just beginning to glow in the morning sky when I woke up on Monday. I heard the sound of Dad's truck pulling out from behind the trailer. I remembered that he was taking Mom to the train station for her day in the city.

About once a month, Mom spends a day by herself in the city, to, get this, get away from all the craziness. It's like Macy's spending a day at Bloomingdale's to get away from all the shopping.

To get away from the craziness today, Mom is going to a UFO convention. It's one of the few places where she seems completely normal. I went with her to one of them once and pretty much everyone thinks they're an alien or that they were abducted by an alien or maybe that they have an alien living in their microwave.

I pulled the blankets back over my head. Wren was starting camp this morning, while I was taking care of Chuck and working in the store. I lay in bed until I heard Chuck rattling around the living area. If I didn't get up I'd pay for it later, so I pulled on a sports shirt and a pair of shorts and went to join him.

But when I got to the kitchen, I could see that I was already too late. Chuck was wearing the same T-shirt he wore yesterday, complete with yesterday's stains, shorts he had put on backward, and one flip-flop. All he needed to complete the look was a pair of socks on his ears.

Chuck had also attempted to pour his own cereal and ended up spilling about half the box onto the table. Now he was trying to get the cereal back into the box, but every third or fourth piece ended up either in his mouth or on the floor.

The sticky cereal crunched under my feet. "Don't move from that chair," I told Chuck. I grabbed the box and scooped the cereal on the table back into it.

"One more minute," I said, seizing the broom and sweeping the fallen cereal into a pile. Then I went to the refrigerator, got some milk, and poured it into his bowl.

He put his arms around the bowl and pulled it toward him.

"Careful, you'll pull the bowl—"

"Ah!" Chuck cried as the cereal bowl fell onto his lap. He hopped up, scattering milk and soggy cereal all over the kitchen before slipping on the heap of cereal I had just swept up. "Your fault," he said from the floor.

"Why don't you blame me for toxic waste while you're at it?" I grumbled, sending him into our room to put on some clean clothes.

After a quick mop, I walked into our room to hustle him along. He was lying on the floor in his underpants and a T-shirt, playing with his trucks. "What are you doing?" I yelled. "I told you to get dressed." I jerked open his drawer and pulled out a pair of shorts, which I threw at him.

"Ouch." He pulled his face into a pout. "I'm going to tell Mommy."

"Come on, Chuck, move," I snapped. "I promised Wren I'd meet her at the gate."

"You're not being nice to me," he whined.

"Not killing you right now is being nice to you," I said. I helped him into his shorts and pulled him out of the trailer.

Wren was already at the driveway gate, nervously pacing back and forth. "Thank goodness you're here," she said. "I really need the moral support."

"Moral support," I muttered. As far as I was concerned, needing moral support to go to Camp Greenlong was like needing moral support for winning the lottery.

Chuck ran over to Wren and began to whimper.

"What's the matter?" she asked, picking him up.

"She's mean to me," Chuck said, pointing to me, "and I'm going to have her headed."

"That's beheaded, sweetheart," Wren corrected.

"You know what," I said to Wren, "if you think he's such a sweetheart, you can have him."

Chuck made a face at me over Wren's shoulder.

She shifted him to check her watch. "It's doom time," she said.

On cue, the black limo pulled into the gates and stopped in front of us.

"Come on, Chuck," I said, reaching for him. "Time to say good-bye."

"No," Chuck said, clutching my cousin.

I stood there scowling while Lance got out and greeted Wren and Chuck like they were his best buddies. He was so happy that it was her turn to go to camp. As usual, I was treated like Invisible Girl.

"I want to go to camp, too," Chuck said.

"It's okay with me," Lance said, patting Chuck's head.

"Well, it's not okay with me," I said.

"She's so mean," Chuck said.

"You want to sit in the limousine?" Lance asked Chuck sweetly. "Come on," he said, bringing Chuck over to the car.

"Look, here comes Blanca," Wren said.

Blanca was jogging down the driveway, holding a portable phone in one hand and a dishcloth in the other. "Miss Wren, your *madre*," she called.

"The last person I want to speak to," Wren said. Aunt Leora still hadn't come back from the retreat and didn't know that today was Wren's real first day of camp.

"Well, luckily she doesn't want to speak to you, Gracie, she wants to speak to me," I said loudly.

"Oh. Right," Wren said.

"Look at me. I'm steering the limousine," Chuck yelled from the driver's seat.

"I'll get the phone and then maybe she'll want to talk with you, too," I said to Wren.

"It's getting late," Wren said, hopping into the limousine.

I began trotting up the driveway to meet Blanca. But, while my back was turned, the limousine pulled away, taking Wren and Chuck, too.

"Hey," I shouted. Blanca and I ran down the driveway after the limousine, but it turned out of the gate. "Stop," I screamed after the car. I saw Chuck stick his head out of the passenger window in the front seat and get jerked back.

"How could they just take off like that?" I yelled to Blanca. "With Chuck!"

Blanca handed me the phone. "You explain your *tía*," she said in broken English.

"Hello, Aunt Leora. No. Nothing's going on. I was yelling about Chuck. Yeah. Wren just left for camp in the limousine." I listened for a moment. "Okay. I'll tell her that you will be back this afternoon. Happy chanting." I clicked the OFF switch on the phone and handed it back to Blanca. "This is really not right. My mother is going to go berserk."

"Mrs. Wright. She *muy* excitable," Blanca agreed.

"Tell me about it," I said.

"Tell her no worry. Mr. Chuck, he safe with Miss Wren."

I calmed down a little. "That's true I guess." After saying good-bye to Blanca, I waylaid Dad, who had just gotten back from the train station and assorted errands, and told him what happened.

"That's incredibly stupid of Wren," he said, annoyed. "But she did it, and now she can take care of Chuck for the rest of the morning. I'm not going to waste an hour driving there and back, that's for sure." Grumbling to himself, he called Camp Greenlong and left a long phone message for Lady

Gregson. "There," he said, hanging up the phone. "If she can't manage, she can call me."

Since Chuck was gone, I went to the shop early. After a Sunday without me, the store was a mess. Dad went into the back to refinish some furniture, while I worked in the front. And the store was hopping, too. Before I even finished cleaning up, I sold a fireplace screen, kerosene lantern, metal watering can, and some red glass jars. And, by the time I was ready to leave, I had disposed of a patchwork quilt, six mismatched napkin rings I claimed were a special kind of set, a pair of painted night tables, and eleven sterling silver dessert forks. I snagged a ride home with a friend of Dad's and was waiting at the Baldwins' gate at 1:20.

The sun was high in the sky, and the wispy clouds did nothing to dim its heat. By 1:45 I felt like I was wilting. I moved under a tree and sat down to wait.

At 2:00 Wren's piano teacher drove up, and at 2:15 he left. More curious than worried, I walked over to the mansion to ask Blanca what was going on.

"Miss Wren no come home. Mr. Piano Man, he leave in a puff."

"Huff. Maybe we should call the camp. Find out what is going on."

"Camp lady call. Want to speak to Mrs. Baldwin, but she no home."

"Let's call now," I said. I reached Lady Gregson and found out that neither Wren nor Chuck showed up this morning. Also, that Lady Gregson hadn't gotten Dad's phone message. This was weird. I called Dad.

"I'm on my way. Stay calm!" Dad shouted, slamming the phone down.

"Blanca," I yelled. "I'm going to look in the tree house and our trailer to make sure that Wren and Chuck aren't there. You check Wren's room to see if she left a note. A, uh, *carta*," I said, remembering the Spanish word for letter.

"*Sí, sí.*"

Worried now, I sped across the Baldwins' perfect green lawn. But a quick search showed that neither Wren nor Chuck had come back. I ran to the gates to meet Dad. But before he arrived, Mom showed up in a cab.

"Thank goodness you are all right," she said to

me. "At the convention there was a sudden crush of people, and when I looked down I had a note in my hand. It said: 'D.W. Go home. Love, N.G.'"

I hugged my mother and began to cry.

"What happened? Where is Charles?"

"I don't know," I sobbed. "I don't know."

Mom drew herself up and took a deep breath. "Tell the Magnificent Presence what happened. Every detail." She put her arm around me and led me back to our trailer.

While I was talking, Dad rattled up in the truck, accidentally banging into the picnic table. "Everybody stay calm!" he yelled.

"Maybe they were in a car accident," I said.

"I already called Beach Bay Hospital and the police station. No reported accidents of any kind. And they never showed up at camp," Dad said.

"Did you report them as missing?" I asked.

"I called but the police told me that was too soon," Dad said.

"You know, Wren was really dreading camp. Maybe she just decided to play hooky."

"Without calling?" Dad asked.

"Not very Wren-like, I know," I said. "Still, she might have thought that we wouldn't worry about Chuck because we know he's with her."

"Maybe," Dad said. "Has anyone called the limousine company?"

"I don't even know what company they use."

"Call them all," Dad instructed. "Describe the driver and see if any of them have a contract with the Baldwins."

I grabbed our yellow pages, riffling through until I found the local taxi and limousine services. I called every company listed, but none of them had a Lance Lyway in their employ or a contract with the Baldwins. Nor was there a Lance Lyway listed in the phone book.

Blanca came over, wringing her hands. She explained that she couldn't reach my aunt. Aunt Leora had apparently disappeared from the retreat and her cell phone was turned off.

"I hope Leora is all right," Dad said.

Mom patted his arm. "Believe me, the Maluxziads would rather shave a shark than kidnap your sister." She sighed. "But why would they take Wren?"

"Maybe they just used her to get Chuck," I said.

Mom folded her long-fingered, elegant hands in front of her and rested her chin on them. "Tell me more about the limousine driver, Gracie."

"Well, he was kind of unfriendly to me. But he really liked Wren and Chuck."

"Did he ask you any questions about them?"

"A few. But I never told the truth, because Wren and I switched places for camp. He thought I was Wren." I could feel my body turn stone cold as it hit me. "And he thought Wren was me."

Chapter 16

We stood frozen for a second as we collectively realized the importance of what I had just said.

"Of course," Mom said. "The Maluxziads think Wren is the princess of Pannadeau."

"Wait. You think Wren was kidnapped? Because Maluxziads thought she was Gracie?" Dad asked.

"It's the only explanation that makes sense," Mom said. "Lance must be a Maluxziad."

"Oh, Dorothea," Dad said, rubbing his head.

"He probably got this job to be on the property naturally and get comfortable with our family. Then, when the time was ripe, he struck."

"What will happen when they find out that Wren isn't me?" I asked.

Mom looked grave. "I don't know," she said. She looked down at her pendant, now ruby red, which was blinking on and off rapidly.

I stared at the pendant and remembered what Mom had said in the store. *Orange for danger. Red for destruction.* "It's red," I whispered.

"We must plan," Mom said.

"I was thinking," I said, "that when Ann said the thing about the horse of a different color, she may have heard it from someone else first. Must have, really. Who says things like that anymore?"

"Hmm," Mom said, nodding her head thoughtfully. "Makes sense. You stabbed her hard, right?"

"Oh yeah. If she was a Maluxziad, she definitely would have exploded. Anyway, you could see a drop of blood on her arm where I pricked her."

"Yes," Mom said. "It couldn't be Ann, anyway, because Wren has known her for years."

I clasped my hands behind my back and looked down at my feet. "This is really true, right, Mom?" I mumbled.

Mom held her head high. "I am the rightful queen of Pannadeau," she said.

"Dad?"

"I don't know, Gracie. I, uh, never really believed it before—sorry, Dorothea—but, uh, Chuck and Wren are missing. And I, uh, think we have to go with it," Dad said, stumbling over his words.

"Thank you, Gallant Consort," Mom said. She reached out for his hand and kissed it.

"I think we need to speak to Ann," I said. "Find out what she knows."

In the distance we heard a police siren.

"I go home now," Blanca said, jumping up. She darted out the door and headed toward the mansion.

"Stay by the phone," Dad shouted after her, "I'll call if I hear any news."

"Sí, sí," she yelled, breaking into a run as the siren got louder.

"The Maluxziads had to find a place big and private enough to land a spaceship," Mom mused.

A white police car pulled up, its lights flashing. Officer Sharpe got out, and moving swiftly, walked over to our trailer. She knocked once on the side of the open door and entered.

"Thank goodness you're here," Dad said. "Have you found Chuck yet?"

"And Wren?" I said. "Are they all right?" My eyes filled with tears.

"Normally we don't look into missing persons until twenty-four hours have passed, but because it was another strange thing that involved Camp Greenlong, I decided to investigate informally," Officer Sharpe said.

"The limousine driver is a Maluxziad alien disguised as a human. He probably kidnapped them," Mom said.

Officer Sharpe swung her head in my mother's direction, then looked her up and down. "I'll do the investigating here, okay, lady?"

"You may address me as Your Magnificence," Mom said. "And we know he has another accomplice in human form."

"And where were you this morning?" Officer Sharpe pulled a pad out of her back pocket and flipped it open. She detached the pen that was clipped to the top of the pad and prepared to write.

"I went to the city for the UFO convention, then suddenly felt that something was wrong," Mom said. "I took the eleven o'clock train home."

"By UFO you mean like Unidentified Flying Objects?" Officer Sharpe asked.

"Of course."

"Very illuminating," Officer Sharpe said. She closed her book and turned to face me. "I need to talk to you, young lady." She tapped her nose. "You're mixed up in this somehow. I can smell it." She sniffed the air.

I was mixed up in it all right.

Officer Sharpe kept her steely blue eyes on mine. "What happened?"

"All I know is that the limousine came as usual, and Wren and my brother got in and drove away. Then"—I closed my eyes tightly to keep the tears from spilling out—"they didn't come home."

"Did you actually see your cousin and brother get into the limousine?"

I wiped my eyes and nodded.

"Can either of you confirm that?" Officer Sharpe asked my parents.

"If Gracie says it's true then it's true," Dad said crisply.

"She lied about who she was, and a fellow camper accused Gracie of stabbing her."

"Officer Sharpe, do you mean to say that you are accusing Gracie Quicksilver Wright, Royal Miss of the Southern Seas and the Premier Princess of Pannadeau, of lying?" Mom asked.

"You're a nut from Nutville, aren't you?" Officer Sharpe said.

"Watch what you say to my wife," Dad said.

Suddenly I remembered. "Blanca, the Baldwins' housekeeper, will tell you that they got into the limousine with Lance. She was there, too."

"See," Dad said.

"It's my belief that the other two Maluxziads on Earth are disguised as goats," my mother said.

Ignoring my mother, Officer Sharpe said, "Gracie, you need to come to the police station for questioning."

Dad took a step toward her and crossed his arms across his chest. "I don't think so," he said softly.

Officer Sharpe grabbed my arm. "If you don't cooperate, I'm going to have to hold you as a material witness."

I wasn't exactly sure what a material witness was, but I knew I didn't want to be one. Turning sharply, I pulled away and sprinted out the door. Running like a thoroughbred, I flew to the end of the property and slipped through a hole in the fence that led to the main road. I knew I didn't have much time before Officer Sharpe got into her car and began tracking me.

"Go, Gracie!" I heard Mom yell back in the distance.

I dived through the hedges of the next estate. Four gardeners were finishing up the neighbor's lawn, each doing a separate task that required very loud machinery. Their truck, which was attached to a trailer full of equipment, was in the driveway. I dashed over to the trailer and pulled myself onto it. Bolted to the top was a large hopper full of grass clippings. I jumped in, then ducked under when I saw the men head back. By cupping my hands over my nose, I was able to breathe.

I felt the weight on top of me get heavier as

one of the men dumped a bag full of grass into the hopper. A minute or so later, I heard the sound of the machinery being put away and locked into place. The truck started up. Once we were moving, I lifted my head above the grass clippings. We were headed toward town.

A few minutes later the truck stopped in front of the Seaside Deli. Two of the gardeners got out. As soon as their backs were turned, I jumped out of the hopper and ran behind the deli into a small parking lot. I began hopping up and down, trying to shake the itchy green stuff out of my clothes.

Out of the corner of my eye, I saw a blue town car jerk into the parking lot. Keeping my back toward the car, I strolled casually over to some garbage pails and pretended to throw something away. The car pulled closer, then I heard the sound of the electric window going down. "Worked on your Eleventh lately?" the driver asked.

I looked over at the driver, an elderly white-haired lady wearing thick glasses with blue frames that were studded with rhinestones. "What?"

"Concertina for Horn in F Major?"

For a moment I looked at her blankly, then I

remembered. My old lady customer. "How did your grandniece like the horn?" I asked.

"Hard to tell as her vocabulary has not developed past 'goo'," the old lady answered, "though I am sure it will bring her many hours of pleasure later in life. I wonder if you still have those lawn trolls? I think about them often."

"We do. Come to the shop. But right now I've got to dash. Uh, appointment . . ."

We heard the sound of a siren.

"Police," the lady said, her manner changing completely. She opened the passenger door. "Get in."

I backed away. But, as she leaned forward to open the door, her necklace slipped out of her blouse. It looked like an upside-down pearl hat pin, same as mine. "Now," she said more urgently.

"Your necklace," I whispered.

"A practical piece of jewelry that is equally at home on a coronation gown or a football jersey."

I got in.

"Down."

I slipped off the seat and under the glove compartment. The old lady threw a blanket over me.

"Here comes a policewoman," the old lady

said. "Watch your head." I felt a soft bump as the glove compartment came down. "I'm going to get a map out and pretend to look at it like a confused old lady. You stay down." There was the sound of some paper crinkling, then a minute later a tap on the window.

"Oh, my, oh, my. You made me jump," the old lady said. "Just trying to get my bearings here on this map. Got a terrible sense of direction. Just like my uncle Jake, may he rest in peace."

I heard Officer Sharpe's voice. "I'm looking for a girl, fourteen years old, short dark hair, glasses."

"Died suddenly. It was a terrible lo—"

"Last seen wearing a yellow tank top and jeans," Officer Sharpe interrupted.

"Who?"

"The girl I'm looking for. Did you see her?"

"I did see a girl in a red T-shirt dress. Oh, there go my glasses. Oh, my. Oh, my." I could hear her hand patting around as she felt for her glasses.

"Lady. Something about you is making my nose twitch."

"I'm sorry about your nose, Officer. It must be my niece's baby girl, a trumpet virtuoso in the making but still in diapers, if you know what I mean."

"Pardon?"

The old lady lowered her voice to a whisper. "She smells like rotten fruit."

"Did you see the girl?" Officer Sharpe asked, pausing between each word like she was talking to an idiot.

"I did see a girl hitching a ride on the highway. Toward Bayville. She was wearing a gray sweatshirt, not a yellow top, but she did have short hair and glasses."

I heard a loud sniff. "Something's not right."

"Well perhaps the sweatshirt was more like a faded black than an actual gray."

"I don't have time for this." A couple of seconds later, I heard a car door slam followed by a police siren.

"She's gone," the old lady said. "What a proboscis she's got." Her car jerked forward, then back as she hit the brakes. "I'm not that expert with these types of vehicles," she muttered.

"Thank you," I said, still under the glove compartment.

"I'll take you to Camp Greenlong," the old lady said.

How did she know I wanted to go to Camp Greenlong? "Who are you, anyway?" I asked.

"I thought you knew, dear," the old lady said. "I'm Nanny Goldstein."

This little old lady was Pannadeau's top-level operative?

Nanny Goldstein must have read my mind because she said, "I'm tougher than I look."

I had a thousand questions, but Nanny Goldstein told me to stay low and be quiet. She needed to concentrate on her driving. We lurched out of the parking lot and onto the highway.

About a half hour later, the car stopped. "You are here," she said.

I hopped out of the car and stretched. "Thank you, Ms. Goldstein," I said.

"Call me Nanny, dear. Everyone does. On Earth, that is."

I looked around. Only a few campers I didn't know very well were in sight. But I knew that it was only a matter of time until Officer Sharpe came back to the camp. Giving a quick wave to Nanny

Goldstein, I raced toward the wooded path that led to the meadow above the stable.

Lessons were over for the day and the stable was quiet. I crept past Stedman's door and went to look for Hart. He was in Cinnamon's stall brushing her beautiful reddish coat. Dog stood in the aisle, watching jealously.

I was never so happy to see anyone in my life. "Hart!"

"Hey," he said, putting down his currycomb. "What are you doing here? And how come your cousin never showed up?"

"I know this is going to sound weird," I began. Then as quickly as I could, I told Hart the story. The whole thing. "So, you see," I said, finishing up, "I think that Ann heard someone else say the thing about the horse of a different color. If I knew who, maybe I could find out who the other Maluxziad is and where they're holding Chuck and Wren."

"Seriously. What are you doing here?"

"You don't believe me?"

"I'm not an idiot."

"I know it sounds nuts. I didn't really believe it myself until I met Nanny Goldstein."

"Uh-huh," Hart said.

"But I don't know what to do." My eyes teared up. "Please, Hart. They've got my brother, and Wren, too. And it's all my fault because switching places was my idea." A tear rolled down my cheek. I sniffed and wiped my face with my shirt.

"Don't cry, all right."

"I'm not crying," I said, bursting into tears. I cried for a minute while Hart stared. "And don't watch me."

Hart looked away while I wiped my face and got control of myself. "I need to talk to Ann."

Hart eyed his old wristwatch. "Okay. Everyone's at afternoon swim. How about I go get her?"

I nodded and Hart took off for the waterfront. I paced around nervously until Hart came back with Ann, who was dressed in a cover-up and sandals.

"Are you all right?" Ann asked me.

"I need to know who told you about the horse of a different color," I said.

"The horse of a different color?" Ann said, her voice rising. "You told me this was an emergency!" she yelled at Hart.

"Come on, Ann, it's important," I said. "When

I was petting Flash, you asked me if I was going to be brave enough to ride the horse of a different color."

"Then you stabbed me, right? I'm leaving." Ann began walking back toward the waterfront.

"Who told you that expression?" I yelled after her.

"Who follows me around day and night?" Ann said.

"Vernon. Of course," I said to Hart. "Vernon's the Maluxziad."

CHAPTER 17

It was about five minutes later. Ann had stomped back to afternoon swim and Hart and I were arguing. "Vernon's not a Maluxziad. He's, you know, kind of a dork," Hart said.

"Maybe the Maluxziads are a dork race," I said.

"Yeah. The evil, alien dork race after world domination. That makes sense."

"The Maluxziads don't want world domination. They wanted Pannadeau because its terrain is mostly shallow seas. Now they want my family."

Hart rolled his eyes. "Listen to yourself."

Thinking furiously, I kicked at the dirt with the toe of my sneaker. "Vernon being an alien would explain his interest in space invaders. And why he was always going off on long hikes."

"Oh, please."

"It might also explain what he was doing by the crop circle."

"He talked about that stupid crop circle all day," Hart said. "How he was going to name it Vernon's Circle, how it was going to make him rich and famous, and how impressed Ann will be when she sees his picture in all the papers."

I wasn't paying attention. My mother's words came back to me. *Has to be big and private enough to land a spaceship.* "Ah!" I shouted, slapping my forehead. "I can't believe I didn't think of it. The crop circle is where the spaceship landed."

Hart expelled some air. "Right."

"That's it. It explains everything, the fireworks, the graffiti on the barn roof, all Maluxziad signals. It's because their spaceship landed here."

Hart lifted his shoulders into a shrug.

"I know it's hard to believe," I said, echoing my father. "But until I find Wren and Chuck, you just need to go with it."

"So, what are you going to do?" Hart asked.

"I'm going to go to the crop circle and search for them."

"You want help?" Hart asked.

"No."

I could tell by his face that he was both surprised and insulted. "Why not?"

I frowned. "Because it's serious and you're treating it like a big joke. Besides, you could get hurt."

"You're trying to protect me from Vernon? What's he going to do—dork me to death?" He started to laugh.

"That's just what I mean. It's not funny."

"Okay," Hart said, pursing his lips together to keep from smiling. "I'll go with you. I promise I'll treat it seriously, but don't blame me if nothing happens."

"You'll need a pin or some kind of pricker. Like I told you, they explode when pierced."

Hart rolled his eyes.

"Hart!"

"I've got a fencing foil in the office. How about I tape a pin to the end?"

"Good. While you take care of the sword, I'm going to saddle up Flash."

"Flash belongs to the camp."

"I'm not asking permission. Someone's got my brother."

"Take Dog. She's mine. And I'll ride Cinnamon. She belongs to Grandpa."

"Okay."

While I saddled up Dog, Hart went into the barn office. He came back a moment later with his foil. "All right. Check this baby out," Hart said. On the tip he had taped two open safety pins. "I have some extras in my pocket. If we don't kill them, maybe we can diaper them."

"No jokes." I let down Dog's stirrup and climbed up. "Okay, let's go," I said.

"Hold this," Hart said, handing me the foil. Without putting on a saddle, he leaped up on Cinnamon. She bucked and twisted for a moment, then calmed down. "It's okay, girl," he said, stroking her neck. "All right. Let's move out."

"You sure she's up to this?" I asked, handing his foil back to him.

"Oh yeah. She's not ready to be a hack horse, but Grandpa and I have been working with her every day. All she really needs now is the right person to love and perform for."

"Where is Stedman?"

"He's taking his afternoon nap. You know the one where he goes into the office to do paperwork and conks out for two hours. And if I'm still gone when he wakes up, he'll just figure that I'm out training Cinnamon."

Dog let out a long neigh. "And that Dog is following us, of course." Hart blew Dog a kiss. "I'll always love you the best, girl," he said to his horse. I felt this weird stab of jealousy.

"Come on." Hart made a clicking sound with his tongue and Cinnamon broke into a trot. I followed on Dog. We headed out of the stable and toward the woods.

Just as we got to the tree line, the sun drifted behind a cloud, making the foliage look dark and foreboding. Slowing our horses to a walk, we entered the woods single file with Hart in the lead.

"Okay now," Hart said a few minutes later. "We're getting close to the meadow." As silently as we could, we rode to the end of the forest. In front of us was a pasture of waist-high grass.

"Look," I said, pointing. We could see a figure squatting in the meadow.

"Vernon," Hart mouthed. On his signal, we galloped toward Vernon. I had never ridden so fast before and hung on as tight as I could.

Vernon caught sight of us, and waved us over. "Hi," he shouted in a friendly voice.

"Freeze," Hart yelled, pulling up alongside Vernon and pointing his foil at him.

Dog stopped suddenly and I almost fell off.

"Where are Chuck and Wren?" I shouted as I struggled to regain my balance.

Vernon stood up, his eyes registering confusion. "You're Wren," he said.

Vernon wiped his hand across his brow, leaving a tiny trail of blood across his forehead. I stared at his hands. "You're bleeding," I whispered.

He wiped the back of his hand on his pants. "Cut myself on a nail before."

I clutched my head. "I'm so stupid. It couldn't have been you, anyway, because Aunt Leora knows your parents."

"Huh?" Vernon said.

A grunting noise came from a clump of trees across the pasture. "You hear that?" I asked.

"Yeah. Kip told me that there was a nest of wild raccoons over there," Vernon said.

"Kip's here? By any chance, did he say anything about being brave enough to ride the horse of a different color?"

"Silly American expression, yes?" Kip said, walking out from behind the clump of trees with Lance.

"That's Lance, the kidnapper," I mouthed to Hart.

Lance and Kip were flanked on either side by two goats. One was tan with big floppy ears, the other was white and bearded. "Dismount," Kip said.

"Or what? You'll have your attack goats get us?" Hart said.

"These goats are highly trained Maluxziad agents. Wolves in goats' clothing as you earthlings say."

"*Baa*, humbug," Vernon said. "Get it? *Baa*. The sound a goat makes. Or is that *bleat*?" He did a double take. "Did you say Maluxziad?"

"With all your talk about crop circles and flying saucers, you don't even recognize aliens when you see them," Kip said.

"But you're a person. And these are goats," Vernon said.

"Remember the dead goats found with their brains missing?" Kip asked Vernon.

"The ones sewn up with teeny-tiny stitches?" Vernon asked.

Lance, Kip, and the goats all nodded simultaneously.

"That you said were definitely not made on Earth," Kip said.

"I don't believe it," Vernon said stoutly. "It's too weird."

The tan goat on the left threw its head up and down so vigorously that it got caught inside the pocket of Lance's jacket. It began flailing around, whacking into Lance as it tried to free itself.

Making an annoyed grunt, Lance untangled the goat and pushed it away. "Unfortunately, being goats and all, they're none too swift," he commented.

The goat that got caught on Lance's jacket butted him.

"Ow!" Lance yelled, rubbing his side.

"Having trouble controlling your highly trained agents?" Hart needled.

"Shut up," Lance snapped, pulling something from his pocket that looked like a black plastic water gun. The tan goat let out a loud bleat and backed away.

"Wait," I said, holding up my hand. "Weren't a teenage boy and his Russian cousin killed in exactly the same way? Brains missing, heads sewn up with tiny stitches?"

"Useless Earth creatures," Lance said rudely.

"Does that mean that you and Kip are using their brains?"

"We don't need answer ignorant Earthling questions," Kip said, snarling. "Let us go."

Lance aimed his water gun at Hart. "Drop it," he said, his eyes firmly on Hart's foil.

"Ooh. A water gun. Now you're really scaring me," Hart said, holding his foil tightly.

Lance pressed the trigger and shot a stream of water out of the gun. It hit a tree, causing it to bend almost to the ground. Hart gasped and the foil dropped from his hand. Smiling, Lance released the trigger. The tree bounced back, like a catapult, scattering branches and leaves all over us. Cinnamon let out a loud squeal and reared.

"Wow," Vernon said reverently. "An alien weapon. What do you call it?"

"A water pistol," Lance said.

"It's a Niagara Eight," Kip said. "One stream of water can, how you say, blow you into the next county."

"Cool," Vernon said as Hart snorted.

Lance pointed the water pistol at us. "Off the horses, now."

"He's telling the truth," I said, dismounting. Hart followed suit. We stood next to our horses.

"Ha!" Lance yelled, whacking Cinnamon and Dog on the rear. The horses took off, and the tan goat with the floppy ears butted Lance again.

"You do that again and you're dead, goat brain," Lance snarled.

"Maybe now that he's a goat, he's become an animal-rights activist," Vernon suggested.

"Using goat brains is big error," Kip said. "We saw show *William Goats* Gruff and mistakenly believed goats had superior intelligence. And we know, humans are fussy about being killed."

"Very fussy," I said.

While he was talking, Cinnamon had galloped across the field. Dog got a couple of feet away from us, then stood looking at Hart. "Move," Lance yelled. He took out the water pistol and aimed it directly at Dog.

"Tell Dog to run," I said urgently to Hart.

"Go. Now!" Hart bellowed at Dog.

Hearing the tension in his voice, Dog trotted toward Cinnamon.

"Walk," Lance said, pointing the water gun at us. "Gracie and Chuck are behind the bushes."

"Hello!" I yelled. "Chuck. Chuck!" But neither Chuck nor Wren answered. "Please be alive," I whispered. I took the last couple of steps and looked.

CHAPTER 18

The good news was that Wren and Chuck were still alive. The bad news was that they were tied up with tape over their mouths. Wren struggled and moaned, but Chuck lay still, his eyes wide open. Lance pulled the tape off her lips, then my brother's. "No need for quiet now," he said. "In fact, a conversation is in order."

"You okay?" I asked them.

Wren nodded her head and licked her lips. "Yeah."

"Chuck?" I squatted down next to my brother and hugged him. "Oh, Chuck," I said, pulling him onto my lap and rocking him back and forth.

Kip spoke. "Gracie Quicksilver Wright."

I nodded. "That's me."

"What?" Kip said, his voice rising in disbelief.

"I'm Gracie Quicksilver Wright," Wren said bravely.

"No. I'm Gracie Quicksilver Wright," Hart said.

"Don't look at me," Vernon said.

Lance aimed his gun at Chuck.

"I'm the one you want," I said, protecting Chuck with my body. "Don't hurt my brother. He's only a little boy."

"Little boy," Kip said to Chuck.

Sounding exactly like my mother, Chuck said, "I am Prince Charles Quicksilver Wright, Royal Master of the Northern Ports and the Premier Prince of Pannadeau. And this," he said, pointing his head at me, "is my sister, Grace Quicksilver Wright, Royal Miss of the Southern Seas and the Premier Princess of Pannadeau."

I nodded. "That's right."

"Hello, Princess," Hart drawled.

Kip made me explain from the beginning. He understood that Wren and I switched places immediately, but it took Lance, who was no genius, longer to catch on. When I finished my explanation, Lance turned to Wren. Scratching his head, he said, "So I've been wasting my time being nice to you since the beginning?"

Wren's face went scarlet. It just goes to show that nothing, not even being kidnapped by aliens, can keep a person from being embarrassed.

Kip clapped his hands together briskly. "Enough. Gracie Quicksilver Wright, you, your brother, and mother are going back to Pannadeau, where you will have a public execution. You will be put to death with honor and ceremony, and your legacy on Pannadeau will end once and for all. How would you like to die?"

"From natural causes."

"You are what they call a wise girl, yes? Well, your mother should be here shortly, and then we'll go."

"You've got Mom?" I whispered.

"As sister comes for brother, mother comes for daughter. You are a loyal family but a stupid one," Kip said.

"So what was your plan?" I asked Kip.

"Get Lance on your property legitimately, have him make friends. Very handsome Earth body, yes?"

"No," Wren said.

"Get you and your brother to go for a ride, capture your mother, and then, when the moon is dark and no one can observe us . . ." Kip pointed his forefinger to the sky. "Blast off for Pannadeau."

"And why here at Greenlong?" I asked.

"Proximity to royal family, private area, secure place to land spaceship," Kip said. He gestured to Lance. "We should kill the others."

"Okay," Lance said, pulling his gun out. He knocked into the tan goat and it butted him on the side.

"I said, don't butt me, you stupid goat," Lance yelled.

"Baa," the goat said, sticking its tongue out at him.

"That's it." Lance turned the water pistol on the goat and shot it, causing the goat to fly through the air. It crashed into a tree and exploded like a giant water balloon.

"You got his goat," Vernon said to Kip. "You

know, American idiom. Uh . . ." He gulped, shutting up, when Kip took a step toward him.

Meanwhile, the white bearded goat was squealing and running around in circles.

Lance pointed his gun at Wren.

"Don't shoot!" I shouted. I threw myself in front of her, clasping my hands together. "Please."

Lance walked over to me and kicked me aside with his boots. "You earthlings are so sentimental."

"Nooo!" I yelled, grabbing him around his legs, which were encased in thick leather boots.

Taking perfect aim, I jabbed him as hard as I could with my Maluxziad pricker, hitting him squarely behind his knees, in the unprotected area between his boots and his long leather jacket.

Bull's-eye. There was a huge bang as Lance exploded, covering me with water.

I screamed.

Vernon stood there with his mouth hanging open. But Hart launched himself at Kip, trying to knock him over. I heard the smack as their bodies collided.

"Prince of Pannadeau!" Chuck yelled. I saw his

still tied-up hands go to his neck and a little glint of silver. He tried to leap for the white goat.

I raced over, Maluxziad pricker at the ready, but before I could get there, the goat saw what was going on and galloped across the pasture. "Mighty Me!" Chuck yelled.

I ran to Hart and Kip. Although Hart was giving it all he had, Kip, who was larger and stronger, overpowered him, knocking him to the ground. Kip saw me coming and picked up Hart, tossing him at me.

We both howled in pain as we went down. Me because Hart was heavy, and Hart because my Maluxziad pricker stuck him in the arm. "Sorry!" we both yelled at the other.

Meanwhile, Vernon had regained his wits and was squatting down, frantically looking through Lance's wet clothing for his water pistol.

In two steps Kip was at Vernon's side. He lifted him by his collar. Vernon immediately fainted.

"Vernon!" I screamed, but he didn't move. Holding my Maluxziad pricker in front of me, I made a mad dash for Kip. But at the last minute, he sidestepped, throwing his leg out and sending me sprawling onto the grass. I felt a searing pain in my left ankle, which twisted under me as I fell.

Hart charged at Kip. Kip took the blow, then grabbed Hart by the back of his T-shirt and spun him around, knocking him off his feet and onto the ground.

I had managed to pull myself up. Holding my Maluxziad pricker steady, I limped toward Kip. But Dog, followed by Cinnamon, got there first. Lifting her front hooves high in the air, Dog came down on Kip, knocking him to the ground. The pressure from Dog's legs caused Kip's chest to get all squished in and his head and shoulders to fill with water and expand the same way it would if you squeezed one end of a water balloon.

In fact, Kip's head was the size of a watermelon. I made it the last few feet, then drove my pricker into Kip's shoulder. He exploded. Dog let out a high-pitched neigh, shook herself off, and went over to Hart, nudging him with her nose.

"I'm okay, girl," he said, wrapping his arms around Dog and standing up.

All that was left of the Maluxziads was a pile of

clothing, torn sheets of thin rubber, two brains, and two thumb-sized fish creatures that looked exactly like Uncle Thomas's red-capped, bubble-eyed goldfish, except that these had a pair of antennae growing out of their heads.

"What are they?" Hart asked, squatting down for a closer look.

The fish creatures shook in the grass. Then, before our eyes, they disintegrated, disappearing into nothingness along with the remnants of the rubber suits and the two human brains. The only thing that remained was some wet clothing.

"Where are they?"

I shrugged. What was I going to say? That they were Maluxziad warriors. That they swam inside the suit and took over the brains of the dead. That they disappeared because of the bizarre Maluxziad philosophy of no loose ends.

Hart picked up the water pistol and slipped it into the waistband of his pants before getting up. "Unbelievable," he said.

Vernon staggered to his feet clutching his head. He stared at the two piles of wet clothing.

"Attempted alien abduction. Wow, wow, wow," he said reverently. "If only I had caught it on film."

I looked at Wren. Cinnamon was standing over her. The horse was pushing my cousin with her head, trying to get her to stand up. "How about untying me?" Wren asked me.

"How about some gratitude?" I answered.

"Thank you," Wren said, "for talking me into switching places with you, lying to everyone I know, getting into a massive amount of trouble, and finally being kidnapped by aliens."

"You're welcome," I said. We both started to laugh. "I guess this is another one of my schemes that didn't work out too well," I said.

"I guess so," Wren said.

"Oh, I don't know," said Hart. He had gotten Chuck's hands untied and was bending down to untie his legs.

We heard crashing branches and footsteps in the woods.

"More Maluxziads?" I said. I unsheathed my Maluxziad pricker, as did Chuck. Hart pulled the safety pins out of his pocket. He opened one for himself and handed one to Vernon.

"When you prick them hard, they explode," I said to Vernon. We stood nervously waiting.

"Gracie, Charles!" a voice called.

"Mom! Mom!" I yelled.

A second later, Officer Sharpe came into view, followed by my parents and Nanny Goldstein. My mother was dressed in her black cat suit. She had a bunch of Maluxziad prickers around her neck, and her crown was cockeyed. She looked fabulous.

Following right behind her was Nanny Goldstein. Like Mom, she was wearing a black fighting ensemble and was armed to the teeth with prickers. Only Dad looked normal in his old jeans and stained T-shirt. Until you looked closely and noticed what looked like a long pearl hat pin dangling from a chain around his neck.

"Nobody move," Officer Sharpe said.

"The Niagara Eight," I said to Hart. Quickly, he pulled out his shirt so that it covered the alien weapon.

"Gracie Wright. You're under arrest. I charge you with the kidnapping of Wren Baldwin and Charles Wright." Officer Sharpe took a pair of metal handcuffs off her belt and securely clipped my hands behind my back. "You have the right to remain silent."

"Don't say a word," Mom called to me. "Not one word."

She didn't have to worry. For once in my life, I had no idea what to say.

CHAPTER 19

"Got you." Officer Sharpe slapped her nightstick against her palm.

We heard a loud thump followed by a scream. A huge flash of light, brighter than any lightning I ever saw, filled the sky. A second later we heard what sounded like an explosion of static followed by a loud electrical buzz.

"What in the world was that?" Officer Sharpe said.

"Stupid goat," we heard a voice say.

"Lady Gregson?" Officer Sharpe called.

"Yoo-hoo. Wren, Gracie," a voice called.

"Leora?" Dad yelled.

I stared at Hart. Torrents of water were streaming out of his pants. Within seconds, he was completely soaked and standing in a large puddle of water.

"Lose control?" I asked.

"Quiet, Princess," Hart said. He reached into his waistband, but the water pistol was no longer there. "It's gone," he said.

I shrugged.

From the other side of the meadow, a tractor driven by Lady Gregson pulled toward us. Sitting next to her was my aunt Leora. Both of them were wet.

The tractor stopped in front of us.

"Ran over a goat," Lady Gregson said, stepping out of the tractor. She was dressed in a wide velvet skirt covered with a dirty gardening apron. In her left hand was an enormous pitchfork.

Aunt Leora, who was wearing casual but expensive sports clothes, spoke from her perch. "I think you might have stabbed that goat with your gardening implement," she said, pointing to Lady Gregson's pitchfork. "The animal seemed to explode."

"Goats don't explode," Officer Sharpe said.

"They do if they're really Maluxziads," my mother said.

"Only four Maluxziads made it through, and the goat must have been the last one alive," Nanny Goldstein said. "So, the light and electricity were the spaceship disintegrating."

"No loose ends," Mom said, nodding sagely.

"Look," I said, pointing my head towards Mom's pendant. It glowed with a beautiful white light.

"White for safety," Mom said.

"Are you all right, Hart?" Lady Gregson asked gruffly.

He nodded and Lady Gregson patted him awkwardly on the shoulder.

Officer Sharpe took a cell phone out of her pocket. "I need to call for backup and to secure the area."

"One moment, please." Aunt Leora climbed down off the tractor. She cleared her throat as she took in the scene. Me in handcuffs, her daughter and nephew still partially tied up, Hart standing in a pool of water in an otherwise dry field, Vernon facing her with his safety pin out, and two horses, one who was standing guard over Wren. "May I ask what you are doing, Officer?"

"I am arresting Gracie Wright for Wren Baldwin's kidnapping."

"That's so silly, Officer. My daughter doesn't appear to be kidnapped. In fact, she's standing right here."

Aunt Leora began untying the ropes around Wren's hands. Dad was crouched down, untying Chuck's legs.

"She was missing and has obviously been kidnapped," Officer Sharpe said.

Aunt Leora put her arm around Wren. "Madame Policewoman. The fault is not my darling niece's. It is my daughter's," she said, making a stern face and shaking her head at Wren. "She did not go to camp as instructed but, instead, hung around the woods playing with her rather"— she looked at Hart and Vernon—"wet and dirty-looking friends."

"And what, may I ask, were you playing?" Officer Sharpe said to Wren.

"The, uh, tie-up game," Wren said. "Right, Chuck?"

"I hate that game," Chuck said emphatically. He lifted his arms and Dad picked him up.

"We weren't playing, Officer Sharpe," Vernon said earnestly. "Aliens were trying to abduct us. I was knocked unconscious and—"

"And now you're suffering from a concussion and babbling," Wren said.

"If you arrest my niece, I will use all of the Baldwins' considerable assets to sue your police department, to say nothing of you personally," Aunt Leora said to Officer Sharpe. "Do I make myself clear?"

"I know something is going on here. I feel it in my nose."

"Your nose needs a tune-up. Because the only thing going on here is a group of naughty children playing hooky together," Aunt Leora said.

Officer Sharpe bent down to look at the two piles of wet clothing. She kicked one of the piles with her foot. "What's this?"

"Laundry," Hart said.

"If I may interject," Mom said.

"Leave it alone, Loony Tunes," Officer Sharpe said.

"Hey, watch what you say about my wife or you'll have me to deal with," Dad snarled.

"Now I'm really scared," Officer Sharpe drawled.

"You may not talk to my brother or sister-in-law in that disrespectful way," Aunt Leora said, "if you want to continue to be employed, an issue that I am wavering on at the moment."

"Do you know your sister-in-law was incarcerated at Barking Tree?"

"She's very delicate," Aunt Leora said.

"She's nuts," Officer Sharpe said.

"She needed a rest and has been a model member of the community for the last fifteen years. Wren, Charles, were you kidnapped by Gracie?"

"Of course not, Mother."

"Gracie rescued us," Chuck said. "From the Maluxziads. They want to kill me, because I'm going to be the king."

"He gets his imagination from his mother," my aunt said.

"And where are the Maluxziads?" Officer Sharpe asked Chuck.

"They're not here because they got all exploded then disappeared."

"It was unbelievably cool," Vernon said.

"They hate loose ends," Nanny Goldstein chimed in. "So all their equipment disappears when they do. Even their stolen Earth brains, because they became Maluxziadized."

"Did you say stolen Earth brains?" Officer Sharpe asked.

"Yes. That's why there's no evidence," Nanny Goldstein said brightly. "The clothes must have been bought on Earth," she continued, bending down to examine the two piles of soaked garments. "Or they would have disappeared, too. You see?"

Officer Sharpe stared at all of us, then unclipped her handcuffs from around my wrists. "You know what I see?" she said. "I see an officer who's had enough. I'm going to quit the force, maybe go into dress design." She turned and walked away.

"If you need a rest, I can get you a good deal at Barking Tree," Aunt Leora called after her.

"Thank you, Leora," my mother said.

"Yeah. You were wonderful, Mom," Wren said.

"Awesome," I added.

"I've been thinking at the retreat," Aunt Leora said.

"You were at the retreat? Blanca tried calling you there and they said that they couldn't find you," I said.

"I had enough of chanting and bells. Besides, Dr. Bosco smells like a muskrat. I retreated by myself at the Hotel Excelsior with fine champagne, caviar, and old Joan Crawford movies," Aunt Leora said.

"Oh."

"And," Aunt Leora continued, holding her hand up, "I did some thinking."

"Yes," Wren said, stroking Cinnamon's glossy shoulder.

"Mrs. Armstrong was right. I have been acting like a social-climbing sycophant. And, Wren, you can go to science camp if you want to."

Cinnamon bent her head down to look at Wren and let out a little whimper. "Yes, horse," Wren said softly, reaching up to put her arms around Cinnamon's neck. The red horse put her head down behind Wren's head so that it looked like she was pulling my cousin in for a hug.

"If it's okay with you, Mom, I think I'll stay," Wren said.

Hart, who had one very wet arm around Dog's neck, smiled at me. "Well, I guess we all know who Wren will be riding."

I wiped my eyes with the back of my hand and smiled at Hart. "It's love all right."

"I guess so," Hart mumbled, turning red.

"I mean between Wren and Cinnamon."

"Me too."

"I'm turning over a new leaf," Aunt Leora said to Wren. "I resigned all my silly committees and am now going to spend time with the people I care about most."

"And," Lady Gregson said, "Leora kindly offered to host a little tea I'm having for the British royal family in October."

Aunt Leora beamed at Lady Gregson. "The royal family is coming to our house," Aunt Leora said rapturously. "Queen Mirabella, the princes Luxemburg and Hastings, and little Princess Victoria."

"My namesake," Lady Gregson said.

Aunt Leora spun around with her arms open. "Have you ever heard anything so wonderful in your whole life?"

"Dorothea's invited as well," Lady Gregson said. "Her majesty, the queen, is fascinated by alien life-forms."

"Well, who isn't," Aunt Leora said.

Wren started to giggle.

"What's so funny?" Aunt Leora asked her.

"Nothing. Except for a moment there I thought the Maluxziads had abducted you, too."

"Really, Wren," Aunt Leora sniffed.

"I'm glad you're back, Mom," Wren said. "Honestly. I wouldn't know what to do without you."

"Oh, that reminds me," Lady Gregson said to Mom. "Don't forget to wear your crown. Queen Mirabella has a weakness for diamonds, especially flawless ones of exceptional clarity."

"What? That thing is real?" I practically shouted, staring at the sparkly circlet that adorned Mom's hair.

"Reality is such a fluid concept," Mom said, rather opaquely.

"But we don't even lock our door," I moaned.

"This crown is part of my being and no one can ever take it from me. Nor," she added, reading my mind, "can it ever be sold."

"By the way," Lady Gregson said, "next Sunday is Greenlong's camper and family open house. I'd love to have all of you come as my guests."

"Thank you, Lady Gregson," I said. "I would love to come."

"Of course you're going, Gracie," Dad said. "Someone has to muck out the stalls."

Chapter 20

It was late afternoon the following Sunday and my legs were killing me. I was leading Napoleon around the little ring for what had to have been my thousandth pony ride of the day. It had rained heavily the day before and the ring was muddy, making walking difficult and looking clean impossible.

Wren had just finished a private lesson with Stedman and was sitting on the fence enjoying the sun. It was clear to everyone that Cinnamon was Wren's horse, so Stedman codified the arrangement, selling the red horse to Uncle Thomas.

Aunt Leora was busy meeting with architects to design a stable and riding ring. She didn't know exactly how she wanted it to look yet, though she's definitely set on turrets.

In the high grass next to the riding rings, Pierce was teaching Chuck how to catch a football. I finished giving a little girl a ride and was standing next to Wren, fanning my face with my hand. After a few minutes Pierce and Chuck came over to join us.

"Here comes Ann," I said, squinting into the distance. "With some girl I don't recognize. That means Vernon should be appearing . . ." I waited a few seconds. "Now." Vernon came in to view.

"He's a little odd, but basically okay," Wren commented. "What he sees in Ann is a mystery to me."

"She's not so bad," Pierce said. "Helped me with a biography paper on, uh, what's his name again, Gracie?"

"Thucydides," I said.

"Thucydides?" Wren said, her voice rising.

"I forgot to tell you," I said.

"Well, that explains why Vernon is helping Ann write a paper on the history of UFOs," Wren said, tapping her forehead. "She gave her paper to

Pierce, thinking that she could butter him up and then blackmail me into writing another."

"Wait," Pierce said to Wren. "You wrote that?" He clapped his hands together with delight. "Boy did I ever luck out."

"So now," Wren continued, "Ann's paper is due and she needs help."

Ann, Vernon, and a petite girl wearing over-sized sunglasses ambled over to us.

"Hi, everyone. Hi, Pierce," Ann said. "This is my cousin Didi."

Lifting up her sunglasses, Didi smiled at the group. She had sparkly green eyes, a big bush of uncontrollable red hair, and small sharp-looking teeth like a cat.

Vernon took a local newspaper out of his pocket and showed it to me. It was a picture of him standing next to the crop circle.

"Ann's Circle?" I said, reading the caption.

"Yeah," he said, looking at Ann and smiling goofily.

"Isn't that nice," I said. "Must make Ann feel really, really proud."

Ann's lips tightened. "Yes. It does."

Meanwhile, Pierce was looking at Didi like she was a movie star. "Hey, Didi," he said, grinning. "How about I show the new girl around?"

"Okay."

"Great," he said, taking her arm. Pierce waved to us and pulled Didi away. "Come on. I'll show you the waterfront first and if you want we can take out a canoe."

"They'll make a lovely couple," I said. "Don't you think so, Ann?"

"Come on, Ann," Vernon said. "Let's take a look at your crop circle."

"I'd rather go to the waterfront," Ann said.

"We need to work on your paper," Vernon said. "Let's go." He started off.

Ann looked after Pierce and Didi, then silently turned to follow Vernon.

"Bye, Ann," I said. "Have fun."

Ann pushed by me. I was leaning against the fence and off balance, so I fell into the mud.

"Hey," I yelled after her.

"Sorry," she called. Then when she got a few feet farther away, "Not."

Wren helped me up.

"What a jerk she is," I said, trying to brush my pants off.

"You're a mess," Wren said. "How about we go to the waterfront for a swim?"

"Yes, yes, yes," Chuck said enthusiastically.

"I've got to work," I said. "But I'll meet you later."

Wren took Chuck's hand and together they wandered across the field to the waterfront. Feet dragging, I led Napoleon back to the stable and removed his saddle. Then I brushed him down and went to get him a bucket of water. The water splashed all over me, and I banged my cheek on a low beam. I checked it in the stable mirror, accidentally leaning against a freshly painted pole. The beam left an angry red mark on my face, and I got paint all over my shirt. I was not, as Kip would have enjoyed saying, a happy camper.

"Looking good there, Princess," Hart said, popping out of the stable office. "Nice perfume. Is it horse dung?"

I smiled. "Yeah. I think it's called Napoleon."

"I sometimes wear that brand, too," Hart said. "It's not everybody's taste, though."

"You know I clean up pretty good. Wear a better brand of perfume, too."

"I see." He took a step closer to me. "It just so happens I need to be in Beachswept tomorrow night."

"And why would that be?" I asked, smiling.

"A funny thing happened. When I was filling out an order for horse liniment, I must have accidentally written the wrong address on the order. It's going to a place called, oh, what is it? Yes. What's in Grandma's Garage?"

"Purely by mistake, of course?"

"Absolutely."

"Hart Stedman, are you asking me for a date?"

"Absolutely."

"Well, you're doing a terrible job."

"Gracie Quicksilver Wright, would you like to go out with me?"

"As a matter of fact, I would."

"Really? Well, what do you know?" He did a little two-step in front of me. "The stable boy and the princess. Who would have thunk it?" We stood there grinning at each other for a minute. Then he leaned over and kissed me softly on the lips.

There were thousands of stars visible in the night sky. I, Gracie Quicksilver Wright, Royal Miss of the Southern Seas and Premier Princess of Pannadeau, was standing behind the counter of my father's antique store. The store was closed for the night, and I had drawn the shades against the darkness. Inside, the light was soft and golden, the only illumination coming from an odd assortment of colored candles and antique lanterns.

I was with my parents, as well as Chuck and Nanny Goldstein, the last remnants of the royal court of Pannadeau.

Mom, who was wearing her crown, raised her hands. "Now, as a token of our special appreciation for Pannadeau's agent extraordinaire, I present to you, Lady Vestia Dumare, known on Earth as Nanny Goldstein, this beautiful set of lawn trolls."

One by one, each of us picked up a lawn troll and placed it in front of her.

"I'm overwhelmed," Nanny Goldstein said. "Overwhelmed and honored."

"Nanny Goldstein," I said. "I owe you an apology. An apology and, uh, a refund. I lied. I never played with a horn as a child and I'm not the first horn at my high school."

"And," my father said.

"And I'm not going to lie anymore because it's the wrong thing to do and it only gets me into trouble, anyway."

"Well, then I have a confession to make, too," Nanny Goldstein said. "I don't have a niece."

"I'll be your niece," I said, leaning over to hug her.

"A niece and a set of lawn trolls," she said. "What a nice planet this is."

Mom looked around and smiled quietly. "It is a nice planet, isn't it?" she said.

Dad uncorked a champagne bottle and poured some for Nanny Goldstein, Mom, and himself. He lifted his glass. "To my wife, the lovely Dorothea. Queen of Pannadeau, and ruler of my heart."

"Hear, hear!" we all shouted.

Mom stood up and bowed her head.

Nanny Goldstein began to applaud and the rest of us joined in. We applauded Mom for a long time.

"Thank you," Mom said softly when the applause finally died down. She motioned me forward. "Princess Gracie, you behaved bravely and honorably. As its last act, the Realm of Pannadeau honors you."

"Last act?" I said.

Mom nodded. "The Maluxziads on Earth are no more, and Nanny Goldstein tells me that the wormhole has been sealed shut. So I guess our home is truly Earth now." She closed her eyes for a second. When she opened them again, I could see that they were wet and shiny.

"Yay, Earth!" Chuck shouted.

Mom smiled down at him, gently stroking his cheek.

Dad put his arm around Mom. "Welcome home, honey."

"Home, home, home," Chuck sang.

Mom nodded at Dad and something private passed between them. "Okay," she whispered. Reaching up, Mom began to carefully remove her crown.

"Wait," I called, stepping forward. "Mom, I have something to say." I took a deep breath and cleared my throat. "Mom." I could feel tears coming into my eyes and I blinked them back. "Mom, I love you. And I'm sorry I didn't believe you, Mom. I mean Your Magnificence."

"Thank you," Mom said.

I took a step back. Then, before she could take off her crown for the last time as the queen of Pannadeau, I held my arms gracefully in second position, placed my right toe behind my left heel, and bent my head. I sank down, doing a deep knee bend with my left knee while using my right heel for balance. I lifted myself up, holding my back straight and dropping my arms in a simple elegant line.

It was definitely the best curtsy this side of Polaris.